Extreme Overflow Publishing
A division of Extreme Overflow Enterprises, Inc
Grayson, Georgia 30017
www.extremeoverflow.com

This is a work of fiction. Names, characters, places, and incidents either are the product of the author's imagination or are used fictitiously, and any resemblance to actual persons, living or dead, business establishments, events, or locales is entirely coincidental.

Cover design by Creations by Donna www.creationbydonna.com
Author Photograph by Dora Photography www.doraphotography.com

Extreme Overflow Publishing titles may be purchased in bulk for educational, business, fundraising, or sales promotional use. For information, please email info@extreme-overflow-enterprises.com.

Unless otherwise noted, all Scripture quotations are taken from the Life Application Study Bible, New International Version.

Manufactured in the United States of America
10 9 8 7 6 5 4 3 2 1

ISBN: 978-0-9885998-2-6
ISBN: 978-0-9885998-3-3 (eBook)

Prologue

As soon as he walked in the room he slammed me against the wall and kissed me in my mouth. He tasted good and sweet like butter on homemade cornbread.

"I didn't think I was going to see you today," he said.

The intense nature of his passion was so strong that it almost choked the life out of me; he just kept kissing me. It seemed like he'd never stop, not even to let me breathe. Like a cow grazing green pastures he nibbled on my shoulders with his teeth and caressed my neck with the gentle glide of his tongue. With his hands rubbing all over my body perpetually, his touch made my skin melt like sugar in the rain. I couldn't lie I wanted him too and my body responded as such. He had it trained to respond with or without any prompts. Although, his presence was prompt enough. I pulled down the zipper on his pants as he yanked off the wine colored negligee I wore when I answered the hotel room door. The dress ripped in half and fell to the floor in pieces. He didn't care though. He just kept kissing me, everywhere, determined to be with me; to be inside of my being, my soul; the only place he was not welcomed.

"Girl you taste so good. How do you do that?"
I couldn't think of anything to say. We were there for one reason and one reason only. There was no conversation allowed. So without words, I relayed this message so that not only would he hear me loud and clear but that he would also never forget to remember.

Panting and heavy breathing took over the white noise in the room as I allowed the front of my hips to grind up against him. Wrapping one leg around his waist I used the motion in my rhythm to search for the angle of his manhood. I needed to feel it like a person needs water in the desert. It seemed to look for me as well finding fate hard-pressed up against my leg growing to reach in between my thighs. Inside me or not, he felt good. But what was he thinking? He should have known better than to try to initiate conversation. This wasn't our first time doing this. Nonetheless, it was a clear indication that there was something about this time that was going to be uniquely different. Then, all of a sudden, he paused. He stopped like a car trying to avoid an accident. For a moment that felt like forever, he looked at me. He gave me the look of a person wanting to be rescued. What was I supposed to do with that? I never felt so uncomfortable in my own skin. I didn't know what to say because I didn't love him. Flooded with emotion everything suddenly felt like it was all wrong. So I made a move to distract my thoughts and break his concentrated stare.

I kissed him for the first time all night; slow, supple, moist. Carefully and intentionally withdrawing from the soft part of his lip, I opened my eyes to see that he was still in his head. His eyes were sealed shut but transparent. I could see he was lost swimming in the majestic of my spell. In closing my eyes to join him I continued to eat the skin of his forbidden fruit just as the strength in his strong arms picked me up and laid me on the bed; I knew what time it was.

All of what we were doing was wrong; and if I thought about that for a second longer, I would have had to stop. I might have changed my mind right then and I couldn't. I had a point to prove and I wasn't going to resist the temptation, now. I wasn't strong enough, or maybe I was too strong in my own will, either way he gave me his whole soul, pouring it all into mine; contaminated, spoiled and devastated. Still he gave me all of him, despite my alternative reservations.

Aware of much more than I led on, I just knew he could feel it but chose to ignore my intentions. I enjoyed the game we played; I was unattached and winning. I wanted to hurt him, at least a little, for all of the trouble he caused. So I played the strings of his heart well enough to make him dance to the music I created.

To be honest though, this whole situation was suffocating me. It's embarrassing to admit that one single man not only ruined my life, he now consumed it. You know what? Maybe I can't do this? Everything is just too deep, I'm in too deep! This time I was the one to pause; pushing him away, so I can breathe.

“What are we doing?” I asked him.

“I don’t know, Nicky. But it feels too good to stop, now.”

His reply turned me on more than words can say. More than knowing how bad I was going to hurt the love of my life if he ever found out the truth. But I didn’t care, not now. I couldn’t, our plan was already in a full range of motion. Grabbing the back of his head with both of my hands I smothered it in between my breasts, obediently he tasted them like candy.

Hell’s fire oozed into my room on the cruise ship of our destination wedding. Like the sizzling slum of hot lava burning everything in its path, I was immune to its scorn. The worst of me had already died from the pain of betrayal turned toxic in an addiction for revenge. A sting that seemed to feel better than the gripping pain of reality which felt like someone cut out of my heart, slit it open, and let the vultures eat away at what was left.

As the maestro of my own destiny, dealing with him was much easier because at least I was in control of which vulture and how many. Nonetheless, all good things must come to end. I promised myself this would be the last time. After all, eventually I did want to live happily ever after with God's blessing; a blessed life with my man; one man. A girl can only hope God would forgive and grant my wish.

I've learned that my biggest problem is that I'm a good looking woman. I've always been; pretty, hot and tempting to most men. For once I was going to use it to my advantage. I can't have my man just cheat on me and get away with it. Not me! That happens to other women. Not the pretty ones. While my looks alone may not have been enough to sustain my man's attention this time, I know one thing; it's going to be the winner at settling scores!

Buttocks in the air, legs split on the floor he knelt behind me. Lust was in the air surrounding the consummation of our union; it was the air that filled my lungs. At this point I couldn't breathe without it. I don't know how.

Penetration was easier with every thrust because I was so focused on getting him back. We bounced, we swung and we danced in the scent of sin's aroma lifting from the bed, the walls, the sheets and the floor, all night long. It was him and me; payback, exactly the way it should be.

"I'm almost there." He said.

I didn't utter a word. I just kept the tempo of our musical performance. I already knew he was about done because I could feel the sweat from his forehead drip on my back; I made him work for it. Purposeful and with intent we were condemned by the curse only the secret of our vengeance could bring. He let out a loud yell; a roar, as I bit the sheets. We reached the moment of climax right before our bodies went limp; finally we were finished.

After we were done I felt empty; my soul seemed to have disappeared, vanished into the air carried by the midnight breeze coming through the window across the room. Chilling our bodies blazing temperatures to an even clammy cool was the antidote to the moment we just experienced. It was the stiff drink you make at home after a hard day's work.

Overlapped atop one another, the moons midnight glare stained both of our skin a bitter navy blue color. His body took up most of the bed; he was a six foot four inch man, spooning my leg. My small body laid next to him flat on my back, unattached. The length of his arm reached over my waist to the other side of the bed and his heavy thigh draped over my leg, very uncomfortably. But it already was what it was.

I stared up at the ceiling fan for some time watching the blades spin round and round while he slept like a baby, like an addict who was high on his fix. It was empowering. It felt good to be his addiction; I was addictive and addicted to the fanaticism of payback. Even still, like many nights spent with him, I felt guilty. Especially tonight, when my man, the one I love was fast asleep just a few doors down the corridor waiting to meet me at our wedding altar in the morning.

Things couldn't be any other way; we were four months deep now. My body craved him even though my heart wanted someone else; that was never going to change. In the sweat of hot sex, juicy and wet it was our routine to drift off to sleep, but I couldn't. I stayed awake all night until I couldn't take it anymore. I sat straight up with my eyes wide open. Perspiration knotted beads on my forehead, fear stricken, sticky, hot, and helplessly stuck underneath a man I really didn't want to be connected to. Annoyed by his presence, I shook him awake. At first he didn't budge, he was all sexed out. It took me a minute, but once he was awake I whispered to him that he had to leave.

"I can't do this anymore," I whispered.

"What are you talking about?" His voice was loud and cranky.

"I'm getting married in the morning, you have to go!"

"What, that never mattered before."

"Well it matters now!"

"But what about us? What about this?"

"Not now. Please, get out!"

"Even after what I told you, you're still going to marry him?"

"The only way I won't marry him is if he calls the wedding off himself! Now go, Terrance, please."

"Whatever, Nicky! You're tripping. Listen, I'll see you when you get back from the honeymoon.

You can't live without me!"

He slammed the door shut and I didn't stop him from leaving, even though I wasn't really sure if he should go. I was used to the hell he brought to my life. And maybe he was right, I don't even know if I can live without him.

The thought of tomorrow gave me comfort to forget about what just happened. Just one more day now and my little bit of heaven on earth was going to be mine forever!

I jumped in the shower thinking about the next day. Secure and proud of my decision to kick Terrance out, I went back to sleep. Soon the sun will toast to my new beginning and rise to meet my love and I in the new morning, at our wedding altar.

Soulgasm
FOR WOMEN

PART 1

...Inhale

Train Wreck

CHAPTER 1

Where are my clothes?

Partially awakened by the sandwich of my pounding headache and stomach growl I lay naked in what felt like another man's bed. The covers ran away from my body and hid at the foot of the bed draping half way on the floor. The bed was damp from sweat and the room was dark blocking the sunlight. By myself, I laid hung-over, slumped over the edge of our bed. I didn't even remember how I got there.

What have I done?

Last night, another failed marriage, gnawed at my consciousness until it was satisfied; buried deep at the bottom of my bottle of vodka.

What am I doing wrong this time?

The arctic chill of reality blew silence in my room and responded in nothingness.

I can't handle being unwanted by yet *another* man! Where are you, Mr. Right? Yea, Mr. Wright . . . I keep trying at this relationship thing and for what? Where are you?

I screamed with my whole soul like I threw the last punch in a boxing match. There was hardly enough strength left in my heart to beat love. Pain gripped the pillow in front of me and held all of my fears while I cried.

I swear life just isn't fair! I did it all the right way; I went to church, I waited for intercourse, well for the most part but even still, where did that leave me? Stuck, unhappy, and dissatisfied with husband number three!

Staring at the blurry ceiling I fell into the familiar wings of depression, for a moment. My last tear chased the hair follicles on the side of my face; it was all I had left. My one tear drop got lost in the feathers of my heavenly pillow as I turned my head towards the alarm clock to see what time it was. With eyes partly open I read the blue numbers on the alarm clock. I couldn't believe it had gotten so late, I never sleep in. The clock read 5:30pm.

Like a man who is raised from the dead, I rose up and got in the shower. Mist filled the bathroom moistening my skin, releasing the vodka vapors from the night before. The rest of my hangover dissipated in the shower steam.

When I'm done showering, hair damp, skin still dripping wet wrapped in my favorite purple towel I stared in the mirror in hopes that I had washed my soul clean. To my defeat, I couldn't see anything different. Next to the rustled covers, looking like hooker sex had run through them, I sat down to lotion my skin. Wait, where's my phone? The darkness was still ingesting the room whole; I was lost in it. I didn't need the light; didn't want it and didn't turn it on. The cell phone flickered like a traffic light; someone was calling me. I should have picked up the call. It was Susan, the Pastor's wife; I missed our lunch date today, but I had to hit 'ignore call.' She was a nice woman and all but what was I going to tell her? I got drunk last night? Yea, right! There was way too much at stake, like my husband's fundraising project. He's been working so hard to put it all together. I couldn't ruin that for him. Besides I didn't feel like talking, not today. Maybe another day I'd put on a mask and dance for the people. Yea, I'll call her on another day. Speaking of calls, George hasn't called me all day! My towel slid off the bed as I almost jumped up out of my skin realizing he never called. I feared only the worst. And the worst was not about to go down on my watch, no sir, not today! Nope! Not ever again, not here, not now, not when it's my turn to be happy.

I scrolled and scrolled through my phone, searching intently; triple checking the call log only to find that there were no missed calls from him. How dare him! Fury and reason collide while the craziness of my old ways hands me a colorful bouquet of good ole' karma; her fragrant smell was all too familiar.

George always called at least once a day to check in with me, so I know he didn't forget. But I wondered, what made today so unusual? Was it something I did last night? From what I could remember, last night was just another boring celebratory dinner with George and his interns who were headed back to college. We did this every year at the end of the summer to congratulate the kids on a job well done. Wait! Now that I think of it, there was this one girl; young, pretty, perky, tight skin, long legs and long dark hair. A few times she pulled up quite close to him at dinner. I drank more wine purposely so I didn't lose my cool over it. But I remember. I noticed it and it bothered me then just as much as it's bothering me now because of all the young and pretty interns she stood out the most. I remember quite clearly having my eye on her closely. I knew something was funny about this girl and now my husband is missing. Note to self: Nicky, trust your instincts. I clipped the last buckle of my black laced *Victoria Secret* bra and threw on a white t-shirt to go with my stone washed *Seven* jeans; the one with the rips down the front of the leg. My sandals were already by the door. Once I reached the door to the garage I slid on my sandals; buckle loose. It was the way he looked at her, like he knew her, what a jerk! It's all coming back to me, now. I swore I'd never see the likes of her again! But that's ok, wait until I find him!

Wait. Calm down, Nicky. You always wild out. You're always ready to set things off. A few deep breaths will help me to calm down. Maybe he has a reason as to why he hasn't called, right? When you don't have any friends, talking to yourself is the best kind of therapy; the only therapy I trust. I need to make sense of this to avoid emotionally irrational behavior; typical Nicky style-blow up! Ok, yea, maybe he had a meeting or something. Let's think about this sensibly, I said to the audience of me, myself and I.

It was evening now. The sun was setting, but I still opened my sunroof as if it were noon. The car was on, humming to the sound of a silent purr. I sat in my trucks leather driver's seat shaped to my thighs contour, adjusting the rearview mirror. I opened the garage door just in case I needed to skirt off in a hurry to find my husband. There is a possibility that something terrible has happened to him. I have to call him, just one more time. George loves me, he'll pick up. My phone was buried deep in my hot pink *Michael Kors* purse, the one with the purple stripe down the middle. Found it! I dialed his phone and put the car in reverse with my foot still on the brake. The phone rang, but his voicemail picked up the other end. Oh, he is trying hard to declare a war, isn't he? He knows how I am. He should know better, but I'm going to give him one more chance. If he doesn't pick up this time, I'm out of here so fast! I dialed. It rang,

"Hi, you've reached George Kalem . . . "

The garage door closed before the voicemail even beeped to leave a message. I sped out the garage like a *Nascar* race driver. Oh, hell no! I'm not going through this again! You'd think I'd know better by now after husband number three, but I guess I don't. The wrath of a woman scorned almost sent me completely over the edge; apprehension surged through my body. I drove faster and faster until I was doing about ninety on the highway. He doesn't know, I have no problem changing my last name back to its original state; before the failure, before the betrayal and before husband number 1,2 and 3; Nicole Walton. If he keeps playing, that's what it's going to be.

Eventually, I ended up at the park. The manicured park entrance was immaculate; flowers, green grass, lovers holding hands and friends walking. It was the perfect place to calm down; it was an even more perfect place to meet someone. I pulled into the first parking area, right of the entrance. Pulling up to the parking area in front of the lake reminded me of all of the times we shared here. I'd never been here without him. Up against the rock, on the repainted bench, and in the grass, my husband made love to me all over this park. Reminiscent of our times I could still feel his breath on my face; we breathed in the air together. I knew he was there, I could feel it.

The waters movement enticed me to touch it, I did. The waters current was strong, pulling confusion closer to me. What was I doing in such a defenseless place, again? Incapacitating rejection plastered itself around my blackened heart; I couldn't feel anything but hurt. All I've ever wanted out of life was just to be loved and be free to love. Instead I was stuck with misery on this rickety park bench, restricted by pain's clasp. I needed some kind of company so I let misery stay. Vulnerability whispered in my ear a sound so sweet that I heard it taste like the vodka from last night, the kind you use to try to keep sane. But today, I wanted to hear something different. I wanted to hear the sound of love.

The gentle water breeze pacified the thoughts of my insecurities. Wherever George was, was where he wanted to be. It's funny because all of the men I've ever been with did the same thing; be wherever they wanted to be, even if that meant they were with another woman. But where am I? Exactly the place I didn't want to be; looking for my man. How does someone like me end up like this, hopeless? That was never my plan. With no alcohol, I needed to be rescued, just for a moment. I needed to forget all about my craving for love and inhale the revival of a love I never had to look for. His love was always and passionately already there.

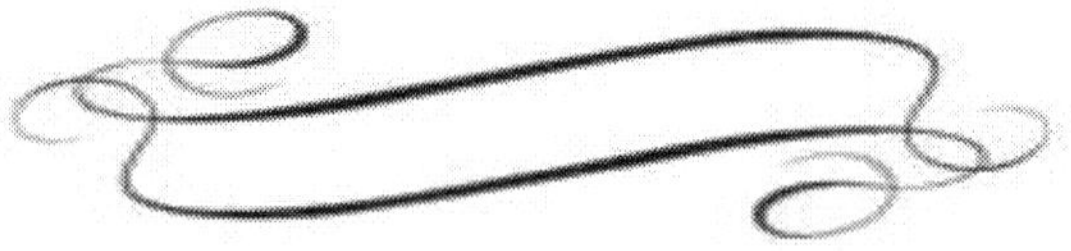

It was finally morning. When I woke up, I touched my skin to make sure there were no more hands. I was hands free with the newness of a bright new sun on my wedding day! I spent the day with my girlfriends getting primped only thinking of him. Then finally it was time to meet my one true love at the altar.

The tender wind moves the black waves of hair cascading down my back. Inhale. I can even smell my shampoo. My hand in his, French kissed and locked together. The sand tickling my pedicure toes in front of the white dress that trailed behind me. Smiling faces stare at us both as we stood on the flower bedded altar.

"You may now kiss the bride," the minister said.

These were the words that erased the past of yesterday and wed us together for the rest of eternity. I yearned for that moment of pure, true love seems like forever. I can still see Hamilton's eyes sparkle with passion for me as he gives my heart rest in the sensuality of his soul. With a firm hand he pushed the small of my back so that my chest pressed up against his body. With another hand he graced the side of my face; near my eye down to my chin and pulled my lips toward his. He gave me the key to his heart and I held his wide back with both of my hands. The embrace kept me from collapsing on the floor, weak from the intoxication of love.

At the intersect of paradise and perfection, we kissed. Our lips parted one another in a smile to the cheering audience who celebrated our union; a spiritual connection that has the power to weaken the best of me, undeniably. There was no greater feeling of happiness then turning around to a crowd of trusted friends and family supporting the bond we shared and demonstrated in front of everyone; mother and Alicia cheered the loudest.

We danced all night long at our reception, but I never touched the floor, my feet didn't event hurt, it was all a dream come true and every time the clutch of his hands met my rear, it made me wish we were alone. I didn't want him to let go, ever.

The evening ended picturesque; a horse and carriage awaited our presence just outside the reception tent on the beach. Hamilton, the man of my dreams, carried me in his arms toward the horse drawn carriage. Friends and family waved "adieu" as we rode off into the sunset. I pinched myself, to find it was all real. My head rested on his shoulder as we rode across the beach back to the resort rear entrance. When we were almost there, Hamilton blind folded me until we got to our hotel room door; I trusted him fully.

When he unveiled my eyes, I was impressed with the scenery and surprised by the scent of the room; it smelled just like Hamilton. I breathed him in.

On the marble floor there lay a trail of red and orange rose pedals leading into the bedroom, the bathroom and the oversized tub; filled with bubbles and surrounded by candles. The reflection of the candle light danced to the reverberation of sincere affection. Champagne chilled in a bucket, next to fresh strawberries cut precisely to fit on the tip of our glasses, adjacent to the tub. Hamilton knew he had outdone himself and I couldn't wait to thank him.

"I have something laid out for you on the bed. I want you to put it on before we get in the tub,"

Hamilton always knew how to show me what I meant to him.

"You want me to put something *on before* we get in the tub?"

"Yes, Nicky. Go and see what it is . . . "

Hamilton was a man of confident mystery; a quality that intrigued me the most. Playfully he gave me a soft nudge out of the bathroom and into the bedroom so that I could open my gift.

Entering the bedroom portion of our suite was like walking into your favorite shoe store with an unlimited budget; so much to see, so much to get into. The suite was huge and the bedroom was down a long hall in the back. The bedroom was decorated in tranquil like colors; browns, blues and greens. The floor rug was almost as large as the room but fluffy, very soft and very white. There were twenty foot glass windows separated by a glass door leading to a balcony that overlooked the crystal blue ocean waves; so peaceful. Even the outside décor matched the inside; heaven on earth. The bed was sunken into the room. As you stepped down into the bed area, the floor was hard wood and the bed was a dreamy white canopy. The drapery across the top of the canopy adorned the bed like a willow tree in the swamps of the Bayou; magically whimsical. I couldn't believe I was there. On top of the canopy bed laid a rectangular shaped black box. I opened it.

"Is this what I think it is . . . ?" I gasped.

Happiness leaked from my eyes as I ran back to the bathroom with the box in hand. I just couldn't believe it. He spared no expense; the bracelet was dazzling.

As I reached the doorway, I looked up, and there he was, Mr. Hamilton Wright, standing in the natural essence of his manhood. I paused in admiration of his silhouette. Quiet and still, he stood staring into my eyes, focused on our love. The tone of his skin and the shadows of his muscular body defined itself. His voice was music enough, raspy and deep beckoning me to "come closer;" the only melody we needed, our love was enough; loud and strong.

Hamilton approached me. His fingers slid down the arm of my satin like skin then interlocked my hand with his, pulling me deeper into him; into the oversized bathroom. When he kissed my neck the softness of his lips caught my breath and held it. The temperature of expectancy released a moan of ecstasy; I could breathe again. In our embrace, we were so close I could taste his skin without my tongue.

Knelt on one knee, he took the box from my hand and removed the pretty pink, white, and yellow diamond tennis bracelet.

"A gift for my, Queen."

I smiled at him with my eyes as he put the bracelet on my wrist. Like the sunrise he rose from the ground and spun me around until my feet no longer touched the floor. With a serpents grip I wrapped my legs around his waist; my arms velcroed tightly around his neck. My buttocks rested in his palm while the dark part of my breast shrunk and protruded through my dress demanding to get close to his chest, they called for him; to touch them, to taste them. All of me wanted all of him, my husband. Enveloped in his being, the reflection of my 4 karat princess cut wedding ring and what looked like a zillion karat diamond tennis bracelet smeared the wall in rhythm and fire. I closed my eyes to swallow the passion in the air; bold and spread wildly through the suite. This was just the beginning of our night as husband and wife.

As my five foot six inch, twenty-five year old

body slid down his six-foot three inch, thirty year old statue of a man, he opened the door and found comfort in the depth of my soul; he made my heart, my body, my being, his home.

"All I want is you tonight, nothing more and nothing less . . . "

There were no words to respond with. I just went with the flow and followed his lead.

Hamilton was not only romantic, but he was down to earth. He could easily stand next to flawlessness in any arena. We drank two bottles of champagne and I laughed until my cheeks hurt. We were so deep into one another that his phone rang almost all night and he didn't even move to see who it was. I embraced the moment to enjoy my husband. And Hamilton enjoyed his wife as we were now one, in love, all night until we exhausted the depth of our passion for each other.

"Room Service!"

The next morning, a waiter brought in breakfast to the suite foyer while the sunlight was just peaking through the bedroom blinds. It was the morning after an unforgettable dream that came true. By the time we finished showering, I could smell the food from all the way down the hall. Hamilton had pre-arranged every moment of our honeymoon. When I heard the door close, I went out to the kitchen area to see what the waiter had brought. My hair was still damp, body still moist, still wet, just a little from our shower.

Hamilton comes out from the bedroom into the kitchen wearing only a towel. I watched his god like figure come toward me and kiss me on my cheek. Even after the peak of our morning, I melted from his touch. He made me tingle just below my belly button whenever he was near.

Hamilton turned on some Jazz music while I brought the freshly squeezed orange juice to the balcony overlooking the beach. As I set the table, I couldn't help but be thankful.

> "Thank you, thank you, thank you God for giving me the type of happily ever after, most women only fantasize about."

"Who are you talking to?" Hamilton said smiling.

Hamilton held a tray of fruit and two fluffy

spinach, tomato, and cheese omelet plates in his hand, setting everything on the table. Adorned atop each omelet was fresh pico de gallo and turkey bacon bits; exquisite to the eye.

Hamilton prayed over the food we were about to eat.

" . . . Amen," we said in unison and laughed, giddy with the innocence of a new beginning.

We ate to the quiet sounds of the ocean breeze over mellow jazz music.

"My beautiful Queen, are you enjoying our honey moon so far?"

"Everything is wonderful, Hammy. You really out did yourself, baby."

"Well there's a lot more to come. We've got scuba diving, waterfalls, dinner, and dancing-all for my Queen because she deserves the best!"

I leaned over and kissed my husband. Hamilton smiled and took a sip of his juice.

Midway through breakfast, Hamilton's smile seemed to have disappeared. His demeanor shifted to a strange place as the sound of him putting his fork and knife down on the plate clanged like the symbols at a parade.

"Nicky, before we get the day started, I need to get some things off my chest."

"Of course, honey. You can tell me anything, I'm your wife.

Hamilton stood up, passed through the glass balcony doors and went to the other room to turn off the music, then came back and sat down. The mood was distinct in its alteration from romance to fear. Then he looked me in my eyes and took a deep breath. The type of deep breath that makes the other person's shoulders gets tense on the exhale.

"Well you know I love you, Nicky, right?"

"Things that follow after those sentences are usually no good, Hammy...what's up?"

Optimistic that the news he was about to share was not as heavy as the weight that had just pulled my heart down to the ground, I stopped eating. Hamilton took another deep breath, stood up and leaned against the white metal balcony railing overlooking the smooth wave of turquoise water below us.

Obviously this was going to be difficult. I'd never seen him in display of such emotional disarray. So I sat back in my chair and waited for his reply.

"As you know the past six months I've been telling you how busy things have been at work."

"Okay..."

"Well about seven months ago Alicia came to me and offered to help plan some of the honeymoon. She was emphatic about making sure things were just perfect for you and I."

"Of course, that's my sister . . . Wait! Hamilton...please don't tell me..."

Hamilton rudely interrupted me.

"Let me finish..."

I could feel myself about to explode, but I cautiously held back the anger that was building up in fear of what was going to happen next.

"Alicia is a very nice person. She is funny too."

He chuckled.

"She came by my office for lunch a few times so that we could finish planning and, well, after a while we got close. Then we got closer and . . . "

"Alicia, Hammy? Of all the people in this world, you hooked up with my sister, really?"

In a devastated trance, I looked beyond him out to the oceans water behind him, although he distorted my view, I watched the water in jealousy of the freedom in the waters movement, wishing I never heard what he said; wishing I could escape with the waves.

"Why wait until we're out enjoying this beautiful honeymoon. Matter of fact, let's take it a step further I mean, why even marry me?"

Hamilton tried to comfort me, but I couldn't let him. I pushed Hamilton away. His touch burned me to my core.

"I'm sorry, Nicky. But it should be very clear that I don't love her. I married you because you are the woman I love. I messed up. I really messed up, But it's over now between all three of us; her, Nancy and me."

"Is it? Wait, Nancy, my mother?"

"It was just a few times, Nicky, I promise. Three at the most."

"You really think how many times you did it

matters to me? . . . But you know what? Now I get it! So that's who was blowing up your phone last night."

He shrugged his shoulders.

"You said it was over Hamilton, so then why were they calling you?"

"I don't know," he said with his head down.

I wanted to believe him, but the contrary is what came out of my mouth.

"You're a damn lie! You know EXACTLY why they were calling you. I bet you thought you would go and see them once I was asleep."

"C'mon, Nicky, give me some credit."

"Give you some credit? I am giving you credit, all of the credit. That's why I said it. So did you go and see them once I was asleep?"

"What?"

"You heard what I said, did you go and see them once . . . "

He quickly rebutted,

"I didn't pick up the phone and I wasn't with anyone but you the entire night."

I had never seen him so flustered. He was mad at me for the first time in all of our four years of dating. His hand gestures were more aggressive than I've ever seen and his body stance was upright and tense. I must have struck a nerve or maybe he could feel my guilt getting the best of me. He rambled for some time. He was telling the truth; an honest confession was refreshing.

> " . . . Did you see me pick up the phone, Nicky? Right, because I didn't. Would you have rather me make something up? Ignoring the call and being focused on you and us, trying to move forward just wasn't enough, huh?"

I couldn't muster up any more words. My thoughts were frozen in a moment and time of four months ago, of the night before last even. I wish I had made different choices.

"So . . . that's it?" He said.

My face turned about eight shades of green as my stomach turned thinking about a few confessions I probably needed to make as well.

"Is what it?"

"Are we all done with that conversation?"

"I am in such shock right now. I don't know what to say. I don't know if we should even be together anymore, I just don't know."

"I realize I was selfish, but Nicky I didn't mean to hurt you. I'm done with them and want it to be just us, from here on out. Just like last night. I'm a man, I'm human and I made a mistake. Let's just move on and build from here."

The guilt of my own confessions prevented any explosion from occurring. All I had left was tears; I cried a river. I felt like I was going to throw up. Why did he have to tell me? Why couldn't he leave it all alone? We could have just moved forward, easily. We were already doing that. Unable to tell the difference between my stomach pain and the pain I was going to cause me and his heart when I told him the secret I was holding; I needed to lie down. Hamilton, the gentleman that he is, followed me to the bedroom and lay with me.

The tender touch of Hamilton's hand soothed my belly aches and mind, almost instantly. He was the one for me. I knew it by his touch. He was trying to make everything all better, and I let him try because I wished that he really could put everything in its rightful place. Instead we were sitting like pigs in the mud of chaos. Saddened by the thought of how very little he knew about the "something" I should be telling him too, I spoke.

"I have to be honest with you, Hamilton... I already knew."

"You already knew what?"

"I already knew about you sleeping with my sister and my rat trap mother."

"They told you?"

"No."

"No? What do you mean 'no'?"

There was no decent rationale I could provide that would give a logical answer to his question. I attempted to respond. He couldn't hear me and I barely wanted him to.

"Well, Nicky? "

"Terrence told me."

"He what!?"

"What's crazy about all this is that Alicia and Terrance are a couple, but they have an open relationship."

"Open relationship, huh . . . Terrance my best friend? He knew I was struggling with this whole thing, for six months now and didn't say a word!" Hamilton paused in embarrassment.

"So when did he tell you?

"He told me like, four and a half months ago..."

The words to follow seemed to have run away from my mouth faster than I could control them. I couldn't believe what I was about to say. I had hoped to never speak of this moment again but here I was, speaking about it. I wasn't even sure what I wanted to do yet. But what I did know was that being without Hamilton was never one of the options I was going to offer. I had to figure out a way to tell him and keep him. My pride wouldn't let me let him go. Even though the sweet taste of revenge began to materialize from within, I remembered last night and licked the vengeance that dripped from the tip of each and every finger before I said another word. I wanted to feel the pain I felt.

Hamilton interrupted my thoughts as he walked away from me over to the twenty foot window in the bedroom area of the suite, staring at the city. I couldn't stand to watch him stand there alone. He had gotten played and was now hurt and betrayed, all because of me well, actually because of him. I walked over underneath Hamilton and he held me sweetly in his arms. He needed me and I needed him, even though there was still more I needed to tell him.

"Well," he said. "Now it's all out . . . So, are you going to forgive me?"

"It depends . . . on whether or not you will forgive me . . . "

"Forgive you? What are you talking about?"

"Hamilton, listen, because there is no easy way to say this, so I'll gotta just say it. Terrance and I might be having a baby."

It was like I hit his head with a brick. Hamilton was taken aback for at least twenty minutes, almost comatose. The love that once dripped from the walls had long left the room leaving it bitter and silent.

Then he spoke,

"Get out."

He didn't yell or anything.

Everything about his tone and posture was dead serious.

"You're really going to put me out, just like that?

Searching for a feeling and the words to describe an emotion he couldn't touch; he said nothing. But weren't we even? How could he possibly hold a grudge against me, his best friend or the child now growing in my belly, who might be his? His irresponsibility was the reason why we were all here? Who is this guy trying to fool? He *owes* me the support!

"So you're saying, there's no way we can work through this?"

"Are you crazy, Nicky?"

"But Hammy, I don't want to be with him. I just don't believe in getting an abortion, that's all. We can't work through this, baby? Who knows the baby could be yours. Besides, neither one of us is innocent. So, why don't we call bygones, bygones and just move forward."

"I don't know if that's possible, Nicky. I can't even stand the sight of your right now. Pregnant?"

I decided to let that comment go.

"Well let's at least enjoy what's left of this honeymoon."

"But Nicky, I don't know if I can. I don't know if I can trust you?"

"What? No, Hamilton, the question really is about whether or not I can trust YOU! You broke the trust first."

"Ok, ok... You know what; let's forget about all that right now. Matter of fact let's go out. Are you ready to go?"

"Almost, I guess. Let me finish getting dressed."

"Alright. I'm going to finish getting dressed too. I'll wait for you in the other room." He said.

Hamilton put his clothes on, a polo shirt, cologne, beach shorts and sandals and waited in the living room. At this point I was in the bathroom putting on makeup.

Shoot! I forgot my phone on the couch.

I walked over toward the living room to get my phone, quiet like the air before rain, looking for hope, expecting the worst. Hamilton was talking on his phone on the balcony. The glass door still open, I heard every piercing word.

"It's all out now," he said.

"We can talk when I get back. Are you still here? Ok, yea! You can meet me at our spot at 8 o'clock. No, where we met last week," Hamilton chuckled.

"...I'll bring the usual, you just bring you....Oh yea . . . this time though, I need you more."

My heart jolted, jumped out of my chest and threw itself to the ground. In menstrual like pain my heart hurt. The nightmare of hearing my husband, my one true love, talk to another woman the same way he did when he spoke to me, like he wanted her the way he wanted me, threw sand on the blazing fire we just shared earlier this morning; good morning sex in the shower. How could he change up so easily and so quickly? Who was this guy?

I inched back to the bathroom on my tippy toes to avoid Hamilton being able to see my phone blink from the incoming message. It was Terrance.

"I just closed on the house! I miss you already . . . It should have been me saying I do to you. But I know I'll see you again. Did you tell him yet? Don't' worry we're going to be fine. Alicia left today! It was . . . "

Immediately I closed the phone. I could not believe the mess I had let myself get into.

Why didn't I just confront him about the affair when I first knew about it?

I couldn't even think about responding to Terrance's text message. I shut my phone and finished applying my make-up. I used the water from my tears to smear the black eyeliner. My foundation was perfect covering for the pinched bruise on my arm; it was all real. From this day forward I would never trust another man or a woman the same way ever again.

Off in a distance I could see a man and a woman walking toward me, I stood up to defend what was rightfully mine; my marriage. The man sound just like George; he stopped and turned to hug the younger looking woman walking beside him. It was the way he held her, I knew it was George. When the train departs the station there's no stopping it. Similarly, anything in my way was going to be run over; I didn't care anymore, I couldn't.

'So this is what you're doing when you're supposed to be at work!?"

"Nicky, calm down. It's not what you think."

"How do you know it's not what I think? I'm thinking that it looks like you're hugging another woman!"

"Maybe I should go?" the young woman said.

"Yes, you should certainly leave, honey . . . "

"No!" George shouted over me. "Please just stay a minute so I can explain." George turned to the young woman and said, "She doesn't know."

"Wait, wait, wait a dang on minute! Weren't you at the dinner last night?"

Gazing through the looking glass of George's eyes I could see that I made the situation intensely uncomfortable. But I didn't care anymore, I couldn't.

"I thought she was an intern from your office? I should have known better than to trust you with them damn interns!"

The young woman looked up to George and said, "No, it's best I go."

"Yes, why don't you do that, young lady? Go home to your mommy and let us adults talk."

The tragedy of Katrina's tears burst through the young woman's eyes. FEMA didn't move; George was helpless, spent from the disappointment covering his face; he had no idea how to fix what was going on. Disillusioned by the lack of amnesty George would never be able to give, the young woman bowed her head, and turned away from George walking out of his life for good. I was glad and didn't care; I couldn't.

The young woman's car was parked right beside mine. George was only one inch taller than I, so I could see the beads of sweat forming on his forehead. He looked like maybe he was about to do something to go after the girl but my train was about to leave the station and he knew he had to choose. His eyes escorted the young woman to her car and watched her leave for good. George was too late. I'm still not convinced he made the right choice.

"Nicky, you were out of line on this one."

"Are you kidding me? You must be joking."

Cynical laughter erupted from my belly.

"No, Nicky. You just ruined it for me."

"Ruined it for YOU? Your WIFE ruined "it" with another woman for YOU? You men are all the same, but that's ok, I'll show you what ruining it for you really is!"

Quickly the train picks up momentum and in my car I skirted off to the house. George did the same but I beat him there, ripping clothes down from the closet now chaotically blank.

"NICKY, WHAT ARE YOU DOING?"

I didn't respond. I couldn't.

"NICKY!"

Fingertips imprinted my arm like a footprint in wet cement, forcing me to look him in his eyes, tears full, heart pained; my soul as good as damaged and only he seemed to love; settle for. I knew it, but I didn't care, I couldn't.

"I'm sorry I didn't tell you this, but that young woman was my daughter."

Embarrassment crept its way up my spine to the back of my head, and tingled. I turned away from him; maybe then I would disappear; the black shell of my heart was cracked, remorse seeped in, infiltrated every crevice until I was warm, flushed, I could feel again, I couldn't escape it.

"Calm down, baby girl. I would never cheat on you with another woman! I didn't know how to tell you and I didn't believe it myself until after the paternity test results we just received this morning. That's why I invited her to the dinner last night, there was a possibility."

"Why didn't you just tell me though? Even if it was only a possibility, I don't understand, why the secrecy? You KNOW how I feel about that."

"I know. I promise I was going to tell you, I just didn't know how to say it. I'm sorry. Her mother just passed away a month ago. Before she passed, her mother told her who her real father was. I wish I had known sooner, before it was too late."

'Before it was too late,' was the only thing that rung in my mind from which the black over my heart began to seal. Too late for what? For who? It didn't sound like he meant me. I'll fix that! We'll never see her again; I am glad. I didn't care, I couldn't.

"George, we've been married three years now, you have to do better than that when communicating with me."

George smiled.

"Fair enough, Nicky. I apologize."

I hate silent pauses, but the air in our hot aired balloon of a room needed it.

"Listen. Why don't you get cleaned up and meet me at the Italian restaurant downtown, *Italianate*? Just the two of us. I'll call the maid on my way so she can clean up the closet while we're gone."

"Where are you going now?"

"Just by the office really quick, I'll meet you there in about an hour."

"Ok."

I was glad he left. I needed some time to think and write. I hadn't kept up with writing daily, but when I did write, my emotions unraveled in the flow and nest of poetic stanzas. I guess Dr. Kim was right. I fought her tooth and nail, but writing really has helped me deal with how I view my problems, I think. After a quick shower, I sat at the desk in the bedroom to write; I only had fifteen minutes before I had to leave to meet up with George; fashionably late, he liked that.

Nicky's Journal Entry

Missing You

Like the moonlight kisses the sea, I wish you could come back to me. I don't want to hear it will be ok.
I just want to miss you in my own special way.
Alone in my room thinking of you; remembering all of the things you used to do.
You meant to me more than words could say.
So the pain of your absence just won't go away.
It lingers every day in every way.

Enlighten me again; entice me once more.
Let me just see you walk through that door.
Let me experience our love once so pure, just once more
On occasion I'm still bleeding
Flowing in the vein of empty feeding, Still wanting, still needing.
I'm still beating, blood that pumps with the strength of our love.

If you could just tell me why, it might help how I feel inside because you know as much as I that…it wasn't supposed to be this way.

Nicky

Lustful Intentions

CHAPTER 2

George had a busy day of running errands scheduled. The sunshine of a pleasant Saturday morning and a big breakfast; pancakes, bacon, eggs, and homemade biscuits with sausage gravy like my grandma used to make for granddaddy, couldn't keep him still. George was on the go and in a rush to get to his first appointment; a typical Saturday.

It wasn't long before I finally sat down to eat breakfast with him that George kissed my cheek on his way out of the door. A chill followed behind him and stayed. Friendly as such, I was accustomed to the distance I stood from appreciation. It had always been quite far and quite cold. Frustrating still, I dipped my pinky in my glass of cranberry juice. I swirled it around gazing into the twists of the liquid. My eyes squinted with optimism, as I watched the tail lights of George's car drive away from the kitchen window. As the lights grew dim in the distance, I stared with hope searching for a sparkle, a speckle, a break light, any flicker of hope that would revive the love we wanted to share but never could find.

> "What were we really doing here? Did he just not get it? Or just not care?"

My appetite was lost in the starvation of wanting the attention of what was supposed to be a blissful union; my third chance. I recognize that you don't get many of those. And mine seemed to be not working.

Blank echoes of an empty heartbeat hummed through the kitchen as I cleaned up, got dressed and headed to the book store coffee shop at the mall. I needed to escape the time between now and George and I's dinner plans later on.

As soon as I got there, I stumbled across a

great mystery science fiction book, so I grabbed it, got some coffee and picked out a small table by the window. Tucked away in a "sci-fi cocoon," with my coffee and reading glasses in perfect location to view every happening in the shop, I was ready to step into another world, one that lived far away from my marital troubles.

There were people everywhere walking in and out of the store. But it was like déjà vu when I saw this one particular couple. The rings they wore on their left hand made it an obvious fact; they were married. The familiarity of their vibe made it easy to absorb into the mirror image of myself; a once naïve young woman, holding hands with the deceitful intent of a young man, attracted only to temptation. The husband's manhood reeked of one on the prowl lurking to find a door of opportunity to bust wide open. Conspicuously conscientious, me an audience of one was fully engrossed. Like a cat with nine lives, I had lived on both sides of their fence.

The young man lead his trusting wife to an

area nestled on the other side of the book store. He even gave her the book to read; clever. Like a lion watching for the weak moment of his prey he perused the store pretending to look at books. I watched his grey blue eyes carefully eliminate the scope of his horizons until he found what he was looking for; she was a pretty doe. He wasted no time in moving in for the kill, stuffing his wedding band in his fitted dark jean front pocket midway to the other woman.

Her fancy was tickled; his loins were intrigued as they exchanged numbers while he walked her out of the store. This young woman immature to the sound of love; ignorant to the persuasion of lust, was oblivious to the suggestions now weaving the fabric of her soul. Yet she walked out of the store with clear hope of a future with him. Probably hoping to marry him! She turned back to see if he was still there watching her walk away, he was. He hand signaled, "Call me." She smiled wide and continued walking. Mesmerized by the infatuation of his aching desire, once my own poison, I was hooked in his plot. I could recite every line of his playbook; I wrote it.

Even as a successful looking woman wearing designer labeled clothing, shoes, and accessories, I've always been guilty of wearing my heart on my sleeve instead of safe behind my chest cavity. The most thorough of washes couldn't get rid of the spell of Jezebel my mother had given me, now a stain on my sleeve; Hamilton was the cause and the only cure. A part of me enjoyed watching what this young man's next move would be; it was better than my book; reliably familiar.

Once the young man could see his prey was dead, lost amongst the weeds of shoppers at the mall, he darted past my table on his way back to retrieve his prize, his wife; who was anosmic to the devious nature the trail of his scent left behind. She was unconsciously buried in the book he gave her to read. From behind her, he tickled her ear with his finger. She jumped, turned and saw that it was just him, and then smiled. She was a beautiful young lady with model like height, ebony dark skin, and eccentric auburn hair. Her style was innocent, fresh and sweet. She was the perfect candidate for betrayal. He walked around front of her and made a show of asking for her hand. Some people cheered while others were not impressed. Even others just watched from afar. Still smiling, she placed her hands in his agreeing to follow in his lead. The young wife's arm was securely fastened around her husband's waist as they walked out of the store. The young man's gray mock turtle neck sweater hugged his physically fit upper physique. His arm was latched around her neck. If you didn't know any better, they looked like they were in love. I knew better.

The young man caught me staring at them and kissed his wife's forehead. He didn't even flinch. Our eyes were still hitched while he kissed her. I wanted to turn away but my eyes were stuck like glue; fixed in a hex, and he knew it. He knew me. A nostalgic trance stared at a reflection tantric in motion, erotically memorable. Kindred in spirit

I knew his game. Matter of fact I wrote the game being played, although he mastered it quite well. An enticing hunger for pleasure was alive and thriving in the air we breathed. He was controlled by it. Even I recalled the sensation of its flavor, an indisputable craving, I thought I had already let go of. The couple glided by me in slow motion and I never got to say goodbye, or good ridden's.

The book in my hands had read me; I was on page five for at least an hour. My reading glasses couldn't fix the distortion of my focus. On every page all I could see was the young man's blue grey eyes. I couldn't get away from him. I had seen, felt and known those eyes, once before.

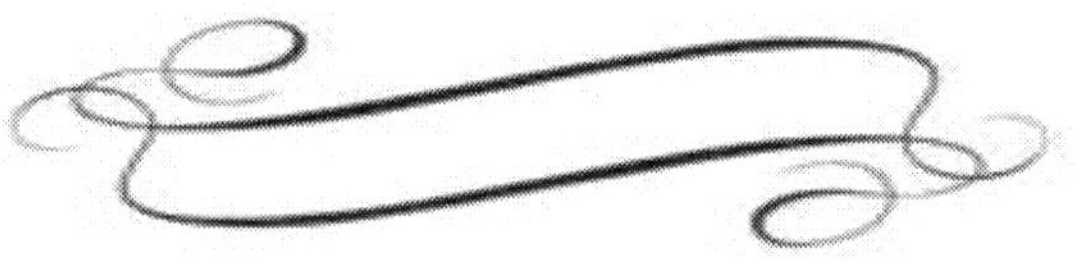

It was my first time at this swingers spot. I had never done anything like this before, at least not on my own.

After the miscarriage, Hamilton and I got divorced; I left him. I knew he deserved better and even though he had betrayed me first, I felt I had betrayed him more; guilty I was, as charged. My fate was the gloom I chose to live in, without him.

The thought of Hamilton being with my sister and my poor excuse for a mother let shadows of darkness seep into my spirit and interlock with my soul; torn, masked and tucked away. I wasn't giving anyone access ever again. I was determined to let my heart shine as black and beat as cold as theirs was deceitful.

"Another sip of my pomegranate martini and I think I'll be good."

A small set of hands rubbed my shoulder.

"Here we go!"

The last gulp of my martini, slithered down, burned the lining of my throat, and slapped my mind silly. It was official, I was *nice.*

"Hey, girl!"

"Oh, Sash, I'm so glad it's you!"

Sasha laughed as did I, but nervously.

"Relax girl, you have nothing to worry about, you're going to like this."

I wanted to agree with Sasha. I wanted to believe what she said. I wanted to save the words from drowning in my scream to get the hell out of there but my mind was louder than her voice. If I had the guts to be honest with myself, a lot of things would have been different. Yet, here I am. Sasha loved this life; she was skilled at it. Her skill ran deep; in the smell of her hair, the feel of her skin and the charisma in her smile. Somehow she knew how to get inside the air you breathed and become your necessity; she was sexy. Men and women flocked to her wherever we went and tonight was no different. After my second drink, even I was interested to play in her garden.

By the third martini I felt pretty relaxed. I began to see more clearly. The room was filled with beautiful people; fun and sociable. It started to feel comfortable, kind of normal; much unlike my relationship with Terrance. Terrance turned into such a bore after he was the one to expose me to this life! Now, I'm convinced that he's doing it without me, so I'm doing it without him. I didn't have a right to complain, even if I didn't like the idea that he was out there because I said yes to it all, the first time. It seemed fun and I wanted to give it a try. Why not, we had the connection? I just didn't want to be with him, like live the rest of my life with him. Our relationship became complicated when he started wanting more of that. He was trying to get comfortable in making me his happily ever after while I was just looking for him to be my happy ending. I didn't hide how I felt but the result was that everything went downhill. He stopped performing; lost his ability to curve the heights of my new found sexual desires. What else was I supposed to do? I had to get out on my own. That's why I'm here with Sash, tonight. I refuse to be alone. Nonetheless, I had made my bed and now had to lay in it; even if I was miserable plotting to soon be rich.

It was Terrance's idea. These days, his best thought towards making some extra money seemed to pimp me out. The perverse perception of retribution led me to accept the opposite of what my grandmother had raised me to believe; a belief I'd lost on my quest for love. Like a kid who's eaten too much candy; his idea made my soul ache. The same idea fueled his anger about me not wanting to marry him; I pimped myself out.

By this time Terrance and I were living together despite many declines of his marriage proposals. I couldn't put my finger on it, but marrying him just didn't feel right. It was just something about him that made him not "the one" for me.

Terrance was a regular at this particular bar. Picking the right people out was his forte; people we would later acquaint ourselves with behind hotel room doors. I had conformed to an open and swinging relationship; everything I was against but exactly what I deserved. The more I did it, the more I disappeared and the more the taste for the compatibility of my skill level increased. For three years now, I thrived in the craving of my appetites hunger; the energy of each encounter fed the guilty desire for love. Impartial to satisfaction, I knew that what I was missing was something I could never have, Hamilton. I forfeited my chance at love for the revenge blinding my blackened heart from seeing and feeling its reality.

"Nicky, snap out of it! Get out of your head and get in the game! Look at all of these people. Can't you feel their energy? It's sexy!"

"I know, I know, but to be honest Sasha, I'm just not into this. I never have been, really. Now, what I am into is being home safe with Hamilton."

"Hamilton? You've been with Terrance for like two years now; Hamilton is over and has probably moved on. Why don't you just marry Terrance? He's asked you to marry him for at least the past two and a half years! Isn't marriage what you want?"

"Yes, but I don't love Terrance! And I don't want to marry any ole body! I want to marry "the one." Terrance and I's relationship was just one of those things, you know? It wasn't really supposed to *be.* It was just supposed to happen. I just wanted Hammy to feel my pain. But after I got pregnant, one thing led to another and now, I've been with so many men, and women, I don't even know anymore . . . this is not how I wanted my life to go . . . "

I almost cried right in the bar.

Blinded by the haze of her own intense sensuality, Sasha never noticed. Maybe this is what grandma meant when she used to pray for a breakthrough to happen. I don't know what it's supposed to feel like, but I definitely felt broken and definitely felt like crying; close enough I guess. I thought I could almost feel something happening, but instead I took another sip of my drink.

"And that's why we're here." Sasha said, "So you can do something about it!"

Sasha leaned over to give me a hug and whispers in my ear, "Girl, forget them both! There is a good looking man walking this way from right behind you."

Before I could turn around, there he was, a tall slender man with caramel sun kissed skin, and stunning white teeth; he was very handsome.

"Hello, I saw you from across the room and was intrigued by your beauty. May I buy you a drink?"

I must admit, he was no eye sore. I haven't seen a man this well put together in at least three years.

"A glass of wine would be nice. Thank you, sir."

He ordered the drinks and brought them back to the table.

"May I sit down?"

"Sure."

Sasha was interested in the group of people across the room and signaled that she was going to leave the table. She was such a natural at this. In a sense, so was I, I just didn't want to be anymore.

"So, what is your name?"

"Kyle. And yours?"

"Nicole."

"Nice to meet you, Nicole. So what brought you here tonight? This doesn't seem like your kind of crowd."

Although I was glad to hear him say it, I laughed to myself and thought about how surprised he would be to know, that at the moment this *was* my crowd; my plot on him was thick!

"My friend brought me here."

"Same here," he said while shaking the ice in his Rum and Coke.

"Listen, if this isn't your thing and I can tell you, this is definitely not mine, why don't we get out of here and go somewhere else."

"Ummm . . . I don't know if I should leave my friend."

We both turned around to look for Sasha, she was gone. No sooner than I turned back around my phone went off, it was a text message from Sasha.

"*Found my set for the night, enjoy! I'll call you in*

the morning."

I looked up at Kyle and smiled.

"That was my friend. She's already gone."

We both laughed and I agreed to leave with him. Kyle was appealing, and although I'd only known him for a matter of minutes, he felt safe.

When we got outside and it was pouring down raining. Under a large umbrella, we waited for the valet to pull Kyle's car around front. He drove some type of shiny sports car. It looked expensive. The valet man gave Kyle his keys, "Thank you Dr. Landrieu."

Kyle nodded at the valet as he handed him what appeared to be a generous tip and we drove off.

We searched for restaurants but couldn't find any we wanted to stop at. It was late and the call of a private affair enticed our desire to be alone and get to know each other better. Maybe it was the alcohol, but I really started to feel like I liked him. He made me feel like I belonged with him.

Kyle lived in a high rise condo loft. The

décor was masculine with beautifully exposed brick on the wall, left of the entrance. I walked over to touch it. He definitely fit the category of the wealthy man Terrance and I were looking for to scheme but the more time I spent around him the more I started to feel like I couldn't do it. He was just too nice to hurt intentionally. I wasn't trying to rob or plot anything on anyone, anyway. That was Terrence's idea. His idea made my soul ache even more. As I ran my hand against the tall, cold, gritty brick wall, I decided that I wasn't going to do it. I didn't want to live as that brick wall anymore.

"Is this the original brick?"

Kyle was in the kitchen pouring wine in two glasses.

"Yes it is."

"It's beautiful"

"Thank you . . . so are you."

I was flattered and needed to hear a man disconnected from everything familiar say that to me. He placed a glass of red wine in my hand and with his other hand led me to the pillows on the floor in front of the fire, opposite the brick wall. We laid on the pillows on the floor drinking wine, talking and laughing. Kyle made me laugh all night. He seemed so attentive, or maybe it felt that way from the alcohol. Either way, it felt good to be in his presence.

We talked ourselves to sleep; I fell asleep in his arms. Like the gentleman he was, Kyle never made a move on me the entire night. He seemed clear in motive which made the night all the more amazing. He definitely didn't share the same intentions I originally had; intentions that dissipated with the setting of the sun. I liked him. He was the first guy since Hamilton that I could actually see myself with, forever.

In the morning, I awoke on the floor of his bachelor pad, got up and went to the bathroom. Washing my hands staring at myself in the mirror, I couldn't believe I had stayed at his house the entire night. Terrance never even called once to see if I was dead or alive. I don't know what I was doing with him; he turned out to be a joke. Clearly he was preoccupied; the joke was certainly on me. However I'd rather enjoy the simplicity of being in love, exclusively, on any day, even if it the feeling was fake and only lasted for one night.

If I never saw Kyle again, I was thankful for the revelation he brought to my life. My grandma would have loved to hear that I had a moment of revelation. She wanted me to be closer to God and I believe I'll get there, one day. However, right now, I going to enjoy Dr. Kyle Landrieu and the wonderful breakfast I smelled; the aroma had reached the bathroom.

Kyle prepared two plates with Belgium waffles, eggs and turkey bacon.

"Wow, you can cook?"

Kyle laughed.

"No, I ordered in!"

We both laughed and ate breakfast.

"I really enjoyed our time last night."

"I did too, Kyle. It was actually quite refreshing."

The awkward silence of anticipation thickened the air with intrigue, interest and curiosity; passion was brewing. Safely staring at the empty plates in front of us, eye contact was avoided. When I looked up to see if he was looking, he was staring at me. I blushed. It was by no accident that we caught eyes. We giggled like second grade crushes. That's when I knew he wanted me. I wanted him too, so I stood up to leave.

"Maybe I should go . . . "

"No," Kyle said as he touched my arm.

The magnetism of his touch intensified the pull that was already drawing me closer to him. We kissed and I evaporated into his being.

We went from fast to furious knocking over all of the furniture on our way to his bedroom. Was this real? Had I found the treasure of love again? My soul longed to be treasured. Although I didn't really know him, I needed him to be him. Everything he did let me know he felt the same. We stayed in his room till evening and christened his place as our home all day long.

Six months later I moved in with Kyle; we were husband and wife. Everything was the way it was supposed to be. I got my perfectly ever after, after all.

Kyle was a good man. He was patient, kind, strong and gentle. He took care of me well, except for the stain of Jezebel no one, except Hamilton, could remove from my sleeve. Agitating my skin, my itch for passion started early on in our marriage. For a little while it had been left unscratched because I was distracted by the feeling of good love. I tried everything I could to scratch it on my own. From toys, to shopping and pornography, I couldn't reach it. Perhaps it was too late. Maybe change for me was impossible. The flow in my fountain of bliss was about to be run over. My conscience now seared from past experiences was still trying to live. I wanted to let love in fully but that itch, it just wouldn't quit.

The jingle of coins falling to the ground

broke my cadence down memory lane, at the coffee shop. I just so happened to have my journal in my bag. I let the flow lead me into an exhaustive place then rushed back home to get ready for my dinner date with George.

Nicky's Journal Entry

Danger Zone

Undeniably we shared a compatible fate. Could he really be my mate? In either way, the eruptions of his soul stirred my heart anew and I thought I heard love.

My entire being fell fast and felt full. Sensuality awakened by a rhythm, we can't ignore, but should run far from experiencing any more.
...Alone again; I thought I heard love.

Every tone in his voice made my lips quiver and my body shake; Searching for something greater; lyrically explosive ...all over my eardrums. Little did he know, he had me at, "hello. "
But here I am alone again; I thought I heard love.

Stop this ride, I want to get off!
Were the words my heart screamed ever so soft.
New suggestions new horizons to explore, it seems that love may have brought his way to my door once more.

Welcome dear love, I implore; cause I thought. I thought I heard your love.

Nicky

Soul Ties

CHAPTER 3

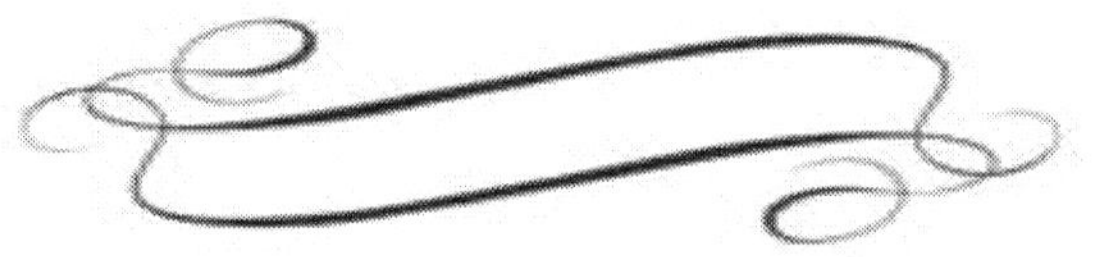

Somewhere near here there is couple making love, there are birds singing and people dancing. But here, right where I am is Alicia and I meeting for coffee in hopes of falling in sisterly love again. We decide to be seated outside to enjoy the spring weather. She still looks good, tall and slender; trendy in dress. I must admit, my sister is beautiful to look at.

"Do you need sugar?" She asked me.

"No, I'm good."

I watch her as she struggles to make eye contact. I spoke to break the silence and not delay this moment any longer.

"It's been a while, hasn't it?"

Alicia looks up from her hot coffee in a cold stare.

"Yea, it has. So why now?"

"Because it's been years since we've spoken, Alicia."

"Six to be exact . . . "

"How can you be so nonchalant?"

"What do you want me to say Nicky? Huh? What is there to say?"

"How about, I'm sorry . . . that would be a great place to start."

"I'm sorry," she responded.

"Just like that, huh? I can't believe you. After all this time, that's . . . "

Alicia pushed me off my soap box with mere words.

"Nicky, get over yourself! We are grown women. You are on your second marriage, after you dumped my man . . . I mean, seriously, let it go already!"

"Your man? Alicia, you have lost your ever loving mind!"

I was so angry, I could barely get my thoughts to make any sense.

"What I don't understand is how you can even think that you are the one who is not wrong! You act like I owe you something . . . What did I ever do to you? I know Hamilton and I aren't together anymore but, how could you do something so terrible, to me . . . your sister?"

"Nicky, you just don't get it."

"Get what, help me to get it. That's why we're here."

"You've always had the richest guy, the most handsome, the smartest . . . and what do I get? A cold bed I sleep in by myself. I haven't even gotten married once, never mind twice!"

"And whose fault is that? Not mine . . . no one told you to become the town whore, or excuse me, the town mistress."

"See you didn't even hear what I said. You

always have to be right, Nicky. Whatever though! My point is . . . "

It all sound like a bunch of hog wash dipped in a pity party, I hated that song. So, I scratched the record.

"The point, my dear younger sister is this, you ruined my marriage and didn't even apologize for it! It's because of you that I had to get married again, it's because of you that . . . "

"Oh please, you're probably cheating on your new husband too."

I stood up and slapped her in the face. Who does she think she is talking to me like that? Alicia's coffee had splattered on the patrons at the next table. I apologized to them as the waiter helped to clean up the mess. My sister still in shock didn't move. I sat back down.

"Listen Leelee, I'll admit I was wrong for being with Terrance, but you started it. And besides you weren't even really serious with him, just like all the other guys you commit to open relationships with. That's what made this different. I loved Hamilton with all my heart. You took away from me the best thing that ever happened to me!"

I broke down and sobbed crying. Alicia watched me cry from across the table with my hand print clearly visible on the side of her face. I let myself have that moment to release; she didn't care, or didn't show it. When I finished crying I wiped away my own tears.

"Thankfully, I got a second chance, which I was also trying to give you."

"You were trying to give *me* a second chance? At what?"

" . . . At an opportunity to apologize!"

"I don't owe you any apology. And after what you just did, you should be apologizing to me!" She laughed, it sound like evil. "But thanks for the offer."

Alicia gets up to leave and my phone rings from an unknown number. Just that fast she was half way down the street by the time I answered the phone.

"Hello?"

"Is this Nicole Landrieu?"

"Yes . . . "

"This is Diana; I'm a nurse at Johnson's Memorial Hospital. Your husband . . . "

I didn't hear a word she said after that. I was just a block away from the hospital so I left the money for the coffee's and ran to the hospital on foot.

Upon arrival, they escorted me to where Kyle's body laid. The doctor proceeded to tell me about the car accident. Kyle died immediately upon impact. My second chance at love stolen from me again! I stayed with Kyle until the hospital made me leave.

When I got home, I couldn't erase the image his body left on my mind. Touching his lifeless soul made me regret everything I had done, everything I had thought and even plotted. I missed his smile, his laugh. I missed the way he smelled and I missed running my fingers through his curly black hair. I missed his laugh and the way the water trickled down the brown cocoa skin on his back in the shower. I was ready to love for real now; I wanted to let him love me and I missed the chance to do so. I cried for an hour uncontrollably because just the thought of Terrance possibly having something to do with ruining my happily ever after yet again, was vigorously enraging. He was so crafty; this was all his fault, all of this! I should have never believed a word he said! With eyes full of tears I called Terrance phone twelve times, back to back, but he never answered. I met up with him about four months ago to try to resolve the animosity between us. Animosity turned lustful; after which I finally cut him off for good. I swear I'll kill him if I ever find out that he murdered my husband.

It was then; on my knees in our bedroom that I wished it was me instead of him. Kyle didn't deserve to be gone, or better yet I didn't deserve to be here.

I scurried through the bathroom cabinets for

something to relieve the pain; something to put me to sleep. I found an old bottle of prescription pills Kyle had from an earlier surgery. There was almost a half bottle left. The knife of regret cut deeply. I just wanted something to relieve the pain, and maybe even escape it. Wishing I could go back to so many bad decisions and make them right, I took the pain killers. I wanted to be faithful beyond the hole in my soul that could only be closed if I fed it with more lust. My mouth full with pills and eyes filled with grief, I swallowed the whole bottle. I could feel my body relaxing, almost as if I were slipping away; finally, relief. I went with it. I didn't deserve to be alive any longer. The torment of my own happenings was unbearable, why couldn't I just change . . . Stop . . . decline? As I began to drift off, I faintly heard something inside me say,

"You have more to live for."

Weirdly enough I listened. Maybe me myself or I was talking to me? They seemed to be the only friends I had. Or maybe I had fully lost it?

Reaching for my phone with my fingertips, crawling over to the couch where it lay. I dialed 911 and drifted off to sleep.

The next morning I woke up to a nurse checking my vitals. I hoped that last night was just a bad dream.

"Is Kyle really gone?" I asked the nurse.

"I'm so sorry Mrs. Landrieu. Yes, Dr. Landrieu is gone."

I waited for her to tell me she was just kidding. I wished it were an evil joke she was playing on me. In silence she finished what she was doing, she didn't look up. I watched her for a sign, an inkling of hope; I got nothing. Once the door closed I laid my head back on the pillow as the TV stared at me. The buzz of my phone against my leg didn't startle me one bit. Expectation was far removed from my life at this point; no one gets a third chance at love. Life seemed hopeless. I hesitated to pick up the phone, but when I looked down I saw it was Terrance returning my call.

"Hello?"

"I heard you were in the hospital"

"Right . . . I just have one question for you; did you do this, Terrance?"

"What do you mean?"

"You know what I'm talking about!"

"Don't try to put this on me! If anyone is guilty it's you!"

"What! Are you kidding me?"

"Don't act brand new."

"You have lost your mind! I told you when I left that whatever plan, arrangement whatever, is over with, just like our relationship. Why is it so hard for you to accept that I am happy without you?"

"Ha! Happy? You don't know happy. Matter of fact, you wouldn't know happy if it slapped you in the face."

"No, you're wrong. I've known happy twice . . . both of which you ruined."

"There you go blaming the world. Nicky, that's all you. You are the only one screwing up your life and every man walking in it. You're no different than me; a natural screw up."

"Speak for yourself! You . . . you just gross me out. I'm hanging up now."

"Yea, ok. You had quite a different tune a few weeks ago."

"A few months you mean"

"Whatever it was, it was good to you, that's why you keep coming to get it."

"What?"

"Nicky, you know you picked up the phone cause really you just want some..."

"What?"

"You heard me and know it's the truth."

"Terrance, you've gone too far"

"Too far? Stop lying to yourself. No matter what guy you end up with I'm always the one who's bed you come crawling back to."

"Don't disrespect my deceased husband"

"I don't ever have to, Nicky. You do it before I even get a chance."

"You bastard! How dare . . . "

"Yea, yea, yea. Call me when you get out so we can finish what we started. You've learned some new tricks in only a year's time of being a part, I wanna see what else you got!"

"You'll never taste this body again, Terrance! I've learned my lesson real good this time, never again . . . "

"You expect me to believe that lie?"

"Oh, it's no lie!"

"Yea, we'll see. When I get you back this time, I'm gonna make you my wife. I've waited around long enough! You owe me Nicky Walton."

"That's not my name anymore, hasn't been since before I married Hamilton, so watch who you're talking to"

"I'm gonna let you have that for right now. When you come back, we'll come up with another plan to get us up some money."

"What!? What are you talking about? Leave me alone, Terrance. Never call me again."

"You say that all the time. I'll call you later."

I just hung up the phone and shook my head. Could he be right? Am I just like him? He might be right, unless I start to do things different, I am just like him. And that's a scary thought.

The nurse came back with breakfast; toast and orange juice.

"Mrs. Landrieu . . . "

"Please call me, Nicole."

"I understand, Nicole."

She set the breakfast on the table.

"Are you hungry?"

"No . . . "

"Well how about something to drink?"

The nurse removed the foil from the top and helped me to hold the plastic cup up to my mouth so that I could drink some of the orange juice.

"Good, you're doing real good, Nicole."

The doctor knocks on the door and enters.

"Good morning Nicole, how are you feeling today?"

"I'm ok, I guess."

"Good, feeling 'ok' is definitely progress."

I nodded my head in agreement.

"I do have some things to discuss with you regarding what just happened."

"Am I going to be ok?"

"Yes, you're going to be fine; although you had a pretty rough day yesterday."

"I just still can't believe he's gone."

"We were all shocked. He was a great doctor here at the hospital, one of best."

"He was indeed a great man."

"You took a lot of pills yesterday. Do you know how many you took?"

"No."

"We had to pump your stomach three times to get it all out of your body."

The doctor paused, then continued.

"In the process you lost your baby. I'm so sorry, Nicole."

"Baby?"

"Yes, baby. Did you know you were

pregnant?"

"No!"

Tears welled up in my eyes.

"How far along was I?"

"About 3.5 months."

"Oh God, No!"

Like free rivers flowing the tears just kept falling. Kyle would have been so happy. The doctor preceded with his diagnosis.

"We've worked things out for you to stay here overnight instead of the psychiatric ward. However, you will be on suicide watch for the next two days. After that we will send you home. That is if you promise to take care of yourself."

I nodded.

I didn't have anything else to say. The doctor touched my arm and then left the room.

"Could this really be happening? Oh my God! I'm so sorry Kyle. Terrance was right . . . I can't even say that this was *your* baby."

It should have been me gone, not him. He

didn't deserve to die.

George just got back from the bathroom and sat down at the dinner table, but I didn't notice him; I was in a moment of dazed reflection.

"I'm back . . . hello?"

"Oh, hey honey."

"Are you ok?"

I picked up my fork and swirled my pasta around in a circle.

"Yes, I'm fine. Just thinking . . . "

"Ok. As long as you're alright, then I'm alright too."

George smiled proudly as if he had won a prize or something, although he really had no idea what I was thinking about. The dinner I dreaded was as dry as the bread on the table. I was glad when dinner was just about over. Why was George always missing it? He paid for dinner and we left to go home.

On the ride there, all I could think about were all of the bad choices I'd made in the past, now in the present. I don't know what I was thinking then. The pain of those memories torched a large space in my mind, so dark; George didn't even notice the smoke, I became invisible like black ice.

As soon as we walked in the door to the house George went straight to the bathroom again. He complained that he might have gotten food poisoning from the restaurant.

I changed my clothes and got in the bed and waited for him with my journal until he returned. I felt so used; and used to being unhappy. I needed to do something to help me get all of this negativity out of me, before it swallowed my soul whole; so I wrote down what I felt.

Nicky's Journal Entry

Faithless

Where am I? Who am I?
How did I even get here?
To the point of no return.
I should have learned…
From the majestic of your words
Dancing on my heart, tearing me apart from the one who really holds my heart; faithfully.

All cause, I loved this man, I hate so much
For opening me up with just…one…touch

Where am I? Who am I?
Feel like I'm going nowhere
Wishing I could undo what's been done right here.

Disastrous fun not worth the ton
of guilt I now bear
I can't even stand the glare –the reflection of my
imperfections; haunting me, indefinitely

All cause I loved this man, I hate so much
For opening me up with just... one... touch

The touch of his hand reached far beyond my sands; an
intangible state, although I couldn't escape
as he made way deep into my inner most me.
He fooled me by introducing me to what shouldn't be
By trade, he exposed infidelity;
in abstract; obstructively.

Purposed to distract my track, marital in color
Hot to the touch, I stayed and played with his distorted
flame, Now there's no one else to blame.

All cause, I loved this man, I hate so much
For opening me up with just...one...touch...

Nicky

PART 2

Exhale…

Guilty
CHAPTER 4

Jezebel had triumphed again; but this time I was alone for the first time in my life. Death and divorce transitioned faster than what I felt I could keep up with.

Tenants were due to move into Kyle and I's old apartment in just one week so I had to finish cleaning. The apartment was bare, like my life; a new beginning, I suppose. Spotless, white glove inspection worthiness still shined with the residue that Kyle was no longer alive and I was alone. A few times I thought I saw him to come through the door with flowers, like he used to do; I wanted him to.

Anxiety made the empty apartment walls seem to be getting smaller; closing in by the second.

"I can't breathe!" I gasped for air.

Where had all the air gone? I ran over to the sliding glass doors and stood on the balcony overlooking the city. Short deep breaths revived the pattern of my heart until it pumped normally.

Out on the balcony, the sun peaked through the sleek metal Venetian bars, I remembered the love lost; there weren't many, but they bruised deep. The more I remembered the more I was reminded of the deceit I had allowed to enter every single relationship I had; killing the greatest second chance to have ever lived. The voices of guilt seemed to be louder on the balcony than in our apartment so I slid back into the apartment weak with emotion.

"Why did he have to be gone?"

What I would give to hear just one more laugh, to see just one more smile and to feel his loving touch . . . At the thought of all I missed and lost with Kyle's absence I leaned against the glass wall that overlooked the city.

"Bring him back, God, Please!"

Remorse for betraying my second chance collapsed my knees as I slid down the wall of the air conditioned apartment and wept on the floor, alone without a husband or a child to hold, I stayed and cried the rest of the day, in sorrowful solitude.

The room filled up quickly with open confessions. The long list of my conquests crowded each other; standing room only. I stood over by the window and touched the Chicago cold glass frozen by the air conditioner. The city was beautiful glowing from the sun set, warm, dim, and fading.

The apartment grew darker with each passing minute. Eventually the apartment was only lit by the shadows of the moon in abstract of the city lights. The day had reached its end. It was over. There was no going back to repeat the day, it was done. I stood up, grabbed my cleaning supplies and locked the door to the apartment holding all of my secrets, free from them all.

In my car on the way to my much more quaint living space across town, away from the hospital and the apartment Kyle and I shared, I remembered Hamilton's face, at the stop light. My passenger seat held the safety of the long stem red rose he had brought to Kyle's funeral for me. But the real question was why was he there? How did he know?

The light turned green and I sped off; debating all of the reasons why he may have shown up. None of which made any sense; all of which made me long for Hamilton even more.

As soon as I walked in my apartment the number twelve blinked on my answering machine and a call was coming in. Rushing to put my cleaning supplies down I was planning to miss the call the answering machine was picking up until I heard the pain in the voice on the other end.

"Hello, hello? Alicia? Is that you? Are you ok? What's wrong?"

"Nicky," she said in a faint voice, "they're going to kill me."

You could hear the flood of tears barricade her voice, she could barely speak.

"Who's going to kill you? Where are you?"

"Nicky, they robbed us and took all of our money."

"Who did? What's going on Alicia, I don't understand."

"Terrance is dead."

"What? Where are you?"

Alicia gave me a slurred address and I flew out the door like a bat out of hell. At any cost, I'm going to help; despite all, that's still and will always be my baby sister.

Cautiously I pulled up to the address of the seemingly abandoned house; the air was still and eerie. As I walked up toward the door people were laying around on the ground in the door way. I couldn't tell if they were dead or not.

"What kind of craziness is going on here?"

As I entered the door way I heard a faint

groan in the distance.

"Alicia?"

"I'm upstairs," she responded weakly.

I tiptoed around the people burning spoons on the stairs. Once I reached the top of the staircase I was met by a nose burning odor and saw a lot of rooms. The doors to some of the rooms were open while others were closed. It was strangely quiet. The first room I looked in I saw Terrance. His brains were splattered on the wall behind him while his body sat on the floor slumped over and leaning on Alicia.

"Oh my god, Alicia! What are you doing here?"

Alicia sluggishly removed the rubber band from her arm when I called out her name. She already looked as high as a kite, and just dropped the needle to what looked like another dose. She must have given into the demon our mother danced with her entire life. Our mother was the most beautiful woman you'd ever see, witty and smart too. Unfortunate for her and us, one poor choice after another including sleeping with my husband, lead her astray from the opportunities life afforded and into the arms of the quick fix mentality. She died of an overdose about a year after Hamilton and I got married. It was too late to save her. And just like mom, it seemed to be too late for Alicia as well.

Alicia's eye was bruised badly and she was half dressed; her clothes torn off of her shoulder.

"Alicia? Can you hear me?

She gave no response.

"Hang on, I'm going to get you out of here!"

"Hey, Nicky!" Alicia said happily, as if nothing was wrong.

She seemed to have lost quite a bit of weight since the last time we spoke, but I'd carry her to the moon if I had to. I struggled to get her frail body in the car. Once I did, we sped off to the hospital I could barely see much of anything driving, my eyes were full. I forgot all about calling 911 to report the abandoned house and dead body. All I cared about was getting Alicia help to keep her alive.

I arrived at the hospital with Alicia limp in my arms; I couldn't tell if she was breathing or not, "HELP! Someone, help!" Nurses immediately took her from me and laid her on a mobile bed. As they wheeled her away I saw that she started to go into convulsions. Frantically more nurses came to her aid and crowded me out. I wanted to help. I couldn't see anything, "what's going on!" I yelled out. A nurse told me to go and wait in the waiting room. The devastation of losing my immediate connection to family was starting to settle in. I watched them roll Alicia away until the doors closed. Then I sat in the waiting room and waited.

Waiting intently for the doctor's response, another family rushed in the emergency room. The unconscious child on the stretcher rolling by broke my heart. Following the stretcher were about seven family members who walked in with bibles in their hand like they were ready for war. All I could think about is what my grandmother would have done, she would have prayed. It had been a while since I even thought about prayer, but I was anxious and wanted to help somebody; I might have been too late for Alicia. Compelled to join the family in their fight for the precious child the medical staff was working diligently to save. As armed forces maybe they could help to save Alicia too.

The family gathered everyone together to pray. I was the only non-family member in the circle, but it felt like we all were one.

Clinching the hands of the women next to me I prayed with the family, sincerely.

Not long before everyone shouted, "Amen!" their doctor hurried in to say the child was awake. The entire family cheered, celebrated and thanked God for what appeared to be healing power and answered prayer. I looked to see if my doctor was coming to give me good news as well, but he was nowhere in sight.

Once the family had cleared out I noticed a man watching me from across the small waiting area. I didn't have enough energy to ask him what he wanted, so I stared back in hopes of him blocking his stare at me. When he noticed I was starring right back at him, he got up and went to the vending machine. I followed him with my eyes, just in case he was crazy. Now, he wasn't a bad looking man; I just didn't want to be starred at, the day was crazy enough.

"Nicky Landrieu?"

I answered anxiously.

"Yes, doctor?"

"Unfortunately, there was nothing more we could do."

"Nothing more?"

A hand grabbed mines. I didn't care who it was. I needed someone to hold.

"When did you lose her?"

"Alicia was pronounced dead at 9:36pm"

It was 9:38pm. I was speechless and just cried.

"Would you like to see her?"

"Yes."

I followed the doctor to Alicia's lifeless body lying on the sterile hospital table. I felt helpless. I couldn't undo what was already done. I was too late. In disbelief I touched Alicia's hand then held it tightly; hoping my squeeze might bring her back to life.

"Wow, this is really it, huh? I thought we'd have more time so you could actually hear me say this to you."

Deeply I sighed.

"I'm sorry. I should have forgiven you when I had the chance, a long time ago."

Regret was the only air I could breathe; it was as thick as her corpse was cold.

"I can't believe this is it. I was sure I'd get another chance. And I'm so mad at you, right now! We promised that if nothing else, we wouldn't go out like mom did. Why'd you have to do that girl, why Alicia, huh? Why?"

I just cried.

"I didn't even know you started using drugs, and now you're gone! Alicia, it's not supposed to be this way. We were supposed to grow old together and yell at each other's children."

I walked in the valley of the shadow of death but I feared all the evil I saw, so cold, all around me. The tears wouldn't stop falling and I couldn't let go of Alicia's freezing cold hands. I stayed with her for thirty long minutes.

"Well sis, until we meet again. I love you Alicia."

I still couldn't breathe, I needed some air. Walking slowly away from Alicia's body gave me chills until I left the room and closed the door. In the hallway stood the doctor, he was waiting.

"Are you going to be ok? Do you have a friend you can call?"

"I'll manage."

"I must say you look awfully familiar.

"Really?"

The last thing I needed at this moment was to be hit on by my deceased sister's doctor. Had he no tact?

"Were you Dr. Landrieu's wife?

"Yes."

"Ok, that's how I know you! We did many

Christmas parties together."

"Ok. Right, what's your name again?"

"Jack Marlette"

"Oh, Jack from the country club, yes I remember you! Please tell Cindy I said hello."

"I will. Kyle was an outstanding doctor and very good friend of ours, so if you need anything, anything at all you just let us know."

Dr. Marlette touched my arm. Wow, I hadn't been touched by a man in felt like forever. I looked deep in his eyes. His touch tried to awaken something inside of me, something that was time to let die.

"Anything at all Nicky, you just call me, ok?"

I looked away, it was dead.

"Ok, thanks, Jack."

When I got back to the waiting room the man from earlier was still there.

"I'm sorry to hear about your loss Ms. . . . What's your name?"

"You can call me, Ms. Landrieu. And your

name sir?"

He shook my hand. "George. I'm sorry are you married ma'am?"

"I'm widowed."

"I see. So it must have been quite a day for you. Would you like to grab some coffee to talk?"

Even through the numbing sting of bereavement my eyes still worked perfectly fine. George was a good looking man. Shorter than my preference, but he was cute nonetheless. I obliged the invitation for coffee.

We sat at a diner and laughed; the first time I had laughed in months. It was refreshing until things began to get a little too close for comfort.

"Ms. Landrieu, I really enjoyed myself."

"You can call me Nicole. And you know what George, I really enjoyed myself too. Actually this is the first time I've laughed like this in months."

"I'm glad. You have a beautiful smile, a beautiful body and soul. It has been my pleasure, Nicole."

"A beautiful body? Beautiful soul, eh? Where'd that come from? Sounds like game!"

"Well, I do have eyes you know."

"Oh I get it, so you just want to sleep with me?"

"What?"

"You know Mr. George, you almost had me. Honestly, I would have rather you just say that you wanted sex right up front. Who knows, I just might have been open to it. And more importantly, I would have respected you as a man, much more." I turned to the waiter, "Check please!"

"Wait, hold on a minute."

"No, that's ok. I've got to go."

"Don't worry about the check, I'll get that."

"Even better."

I couldn't scoot out of the booth fast enough.

"Maybe we can see each other again, on a better day."

"Wow, you are really, just . . . wow. I think

we've already shared too much!"

Was my car parked this far away before? Why is he following me?

I walked faster and faster until I reached the car. He followed my every step asking all types of questions I didn't want to hear. I slammed the car door shut and sped off in fury.

"As if this day wasn't bad enough!"

In the comfort of my own place, overwhelmed by the dish death had delivered, I poured myself a large glass of wine. Sipping slowly staring serenely at the remnant of Hamilton in my new apartment; the long stem red rose from the funeral, wondering what life would be like if I had stayed with him.

Holding the rose as a microphone to the sad slow jams that played through my iPod speakers, I continued to pour more wine. By my third glass of the fourth bottle; I was inspired to write. Laid out on my white leather couch I crawled to the coffee table, grabbed my journal and pen and wrote how I felt.

Nicky's Journal Entry

MISERY LOVES COMPANY

A devourer searches for my soul to eat it alive.
It's all my fault because I gave him the key to my inside.
I left the signs that led him to my soul, to torment, to torch, to remember me no more.

Opened is the way he left the door to my heart.
The stampede of misery tore it apart.
Demise ran the bath water as soon as they moved in.

I backed and breast stroked in the semen of his lies,
Birthing the babies of his seed; swimming anxiously inside
Awaiting the contamination of the fruit my womb bears; venomous love.
Rebirth unearthed is how I remain, overwhelmed from the pain of the inevitable; one lonely dame.

...But it's all my fault because I am the only one who gave the devourer the key that let them all in to my heart.

Nicky

Crossed the Line

CHAPTER 5

George traveled a lot. He did great work with and for the community. After eight years of marriage and two years of dating, I usually labored in the community with him but sometimes I just couldn't go.

Frequently and as a passed time I would coordinate networking and lunch meetings with both men and women. It was a great way to get out of the house, meet new people, and stay active in the community. Between my lunches and his schedule of volunteering and speaking engagements I was often left bored with idol time to spare. I was confident in what my boundaries were and practiced them regularly. I had to; it was the nature of how we lived. After all, the old me died at the hospital with Alicia. So in my mind, today was no different.

"He's late, or maybe he decided not to come."

I watched the door in anticipation. Thirty minutes passed. He still had not arrived, so I decided to stay and eat since I was actually hungry now; no longer nervous.

"It was probably best he did not show up, with George out of town and all."

I blotted my mouth on both sides, paid my bill and left the waitress a nice tip. There was no reason to rush to get home; George wouldn't be there until tomorrow night, so I stopped in the ladies to refresh my make-up before deciding on what else I could do.

While washing my hands I noticed a stain on my new favorite and beautiful yellow dress. Water didn't work.

"Well, I guess I'm going back to the mall to shop."

Coming out of the bathroom I gasped like the wind got knocked out of me, there he was.

"Hamilton! I didn't think you'd make it."

He didn't say anything. He held me tightly in his arms. I stayed there.

"It's so good to see you, Nicky."

I didn't think it would be this difficult to meet up with him. In my mind, this was just a casual lunch between friends. Last month George and I went to the Broadway show, *Fela* that came to town. After we got to our seats I went to get popcorn for George and I and there he was. He looked just as surprised as I did to see him. Hamilton, his date, George and I ended up going to dinner after the show. We all had a great time that night and made plans to meet again soon. Today was the perfect day for a nice lunch with an old friend. The butterflies in my stomach let me know I really felt something else; I couldn't hide it. But I had made these plans before I knew George would be out of town. It was too late to change things now. Besides, after seeing him, I didn't want to leave.

"It's really good to see you too, Hammy. It's been what, ten years?"

"Something like that . . . "

He just stared at me. He could always look in my eyes and see right into my soul so I opened the windows wide to let in the warmth of light his soul brought to mine.

"Do you have to go?"

My feet wouldn't move an inch and my lips answered before I could reply as the wife I had become.

"No, do you want to talk?"

"I just want to be near you. No sex, I just need to be close to you. Even if this has to be the last time. I really miss you, Nicky."

Never any bull, with Hamilton. I loved that. He said what he felt and meant it. He squeezed me closer to his body and it took all of the strength in me to hold my panties up; panting for the passion in his pleasure; a desire that was twice removed from my current marriage and apparently had never died between Hamilton and I. In his arms felt like home, a place I hadn't been in years. We enjoyed a day together; walking, talking, and laughing now watching the sunset from the hood of my car. After a hard day's work of resisting temptation, we were hungry and decided to grab something to eat together.

There was no doubt; I was all in; all of my heart, mind and soul; all of me. But as much as I yearned to experience the totality of his being I expressed restraint. In contrast I didn't have enough strength to just walk away. I couldn't leave and didn't want to; it was Heaven on Earth, right in front of my car, pressed against each other, in the dark.

"Nicky, I never wanted things to be this way."

"Neither did I Hamilton."

"I have always envisioned you as my only wife. I know saying so may have crossed the line but . . . "

I interrupted; my emotions just flowed that way.

"To be honest with you, I wish I'd never left you. It's been the worst decision I've made yet."

Hamilton stroked my arm up and down.

"It feels good to hear you say that, Nicky."

"It feels good to see you again. Hammy"

Hamilton touched my face and laid my head on his chest while I wrapped my arms around his neck. Sensual infatuation escalated quickly between us and before I knew it, Hamilton's other hand was massaging my upper back. The more he rubbed the closer the tip of his thumb got to grazing the side of my breast under my arm. He knew how to touch me so not to alarm me. As foreign as his touch was from that of my husband, I was very comfortable with how he made my body feel. I wanted him to touch me more. As he always could, he read my mind.

Hamilton's fingers journeyed further down my body clutching both sides of my waist, sliding me up and down his body. My private parts whined for the friction he initiated; leaking liquid pleasure. It was seemingly intuitive how well he knew my body. Even after all of these years he was able to stir up a sexual stimulation that set my soul on fire; my husband couldn't even do that. I had missed the feeling more than I realized. Clearly I was neglecting myself from it; from me.

I wanted to ride him like the see saw on the playground, up and down, fast then faster until we were both bumping so hard and gliding so high we reached the sky. Raging chemistry pumped the blood into the erection he had leaning against me. If he put it in, I wouldn't have had strength enough to stop him. I missed him so much. I missed what we could have been and started to regret every second I had spent without him.

His voice beat on my eardrum and pulsated down my backside: making me push it out a little more. But he knew what to do; he held it in his hands squeezing it and lifting me off the ground. Automatically my legs went up and wrapped themselves around his waist. It felt like our honeymoon all over again. Except this time he wasn't my husband.

"Hammy, maybe this is too much. I don't think I can handle having just a piece of you."

"Maybe you're right. I guess we'll always be some kind of irresistible."

We laughed. He put me down and stepped back never letting go of my hand.

"Thank you for a wonderful night, Hamilton. I almost forgot what it felt like to be held like that. It felt like love."

"Have no doubts my Queen, it is love."

"You're making this really difficult."

"Who me?"

His sly smile turned me on, just that fast; he kept me fully engaged.

"Stop, Hamilton!"

"Stop what? Telling the truth? I love you girl!"

"Don't say that!"

That would have made me have to say it back. I already wanted to. I didn't need any more temptation. While I had probably already failed fidelity in its simplest form, hearing that he felt the same way I did, after all these years was good enough.

"I'll never stop loving you, Nicky, I can't do that, I already tried. It's impossible."

"You have no idea Hammy."

I moved closer to him. I wanted to kiss him but that definitely would have been crossing the line.

"Nicky, my life is impossible without you, without love being us."

"Oh, Hammy."

My heart skipped five beats.

"Why won't you come back to me? Come home, Nicky . . . "

"You don't think I want to? Do you know how hard this is? Especially after tonight! I want you more than I can deal with right now. There has never been a love like ours, believe me-I've tried to find it."

"So then what are you waiting for? Because if you had a love that even stood a candle against ours, you wouldn't be here."

"Play nice, Hammy."

"What kind of joker are you with anyway? He hasn't called for you the whole day! He just let's you roll in the streets by yourself? What kind of man is that?"

"He is out of town on business, Hammy."

"See, what are the odds of that? Or did you plan tonight on purpose?"

"Actually, his trip just came up or so he says. We planned this at least a few weeks ago, right?"

"It doesn't matter, really. We're here as fate would have it, why not give us a chance?"

"You expect me to just up and leave this guy? Just walk away, just like that?"

"I'm just saying, Nicky, why deprive our love from existing?"

He was right. His love was home, why am I running from home?

"Because I, well, because . . . "

Hamilton let go of my hands; we disconnected.

"Because, what?"

"Listen Hamilton, you will always have a special place in my heart, always, isn't that enough?"

"No! Leave him like you left me, heartless and without explanation. I would have worked through anything with you Nicky, that's what love does-it finds a way."

I had no words. I never thought about how he felt when I left. I knew the reasons why I had left, but I never knew or even thought about how he might feel *because* I left. Honestly, I thought he'd get over it, eventually. I searched for words to say in that moment, but my mind was a blank canvas; I had nothing and said the same.

"Alright, Nicky, if that's what you want..."

"It's not what I want, I just don't know any other way . . . "

"No other way, huh? I can find a million ways. But you have to be willing to see them for yourself."

I was disappointing him again, except this

time I knew it; pain struck my body like lighting.

"You are an amazing woman. It's getting late although it seems like we have more to discuss. The fire still blazes strong, wouldn't you agree?

"My honest answer?"

"No! Save that for our next talk!"

We laughed and I finally got in my car.

"Be safe driving home, ok?"

"Ok."

He was right. Our love was still alive and intensely strong. Why couldn't I just have him; he's all I've ever wanted, anyway? What's so wrong about that?

In awe, of how it all felt so natural, I realized I couldn't resist, I wanted him, forever. As I picked up the phone to call Hamilton and tell him to turn around, George called my phone; I answered my husband's call.

George rambled with excitement about his busy day and all of the people he helped and about all of the people who needed him. I listened as I always did. My anxieties about Hamilton simmered to a luke warm sensation. George talked until he was exhausted and went to bed. He never asked where I was, what I did that day or if I was ok, by myself, nothing. He rambled with diarrhea of the mouth then hung up. A few moments to myself was nothing short of a tease; I spent the entire night dancing with temptation. After wrestling, battling and fighting the urge to call Hamilton, I fell asleep with a pillow between my legs phone in hand clinging to the corrupt thoughts of Hamilton and I together again.

The night came and went. It was a new day, the day George was coming home. It wasn't long before the aroma of a home cooked meal filled our home and complimented the smells of a clean house and deliciously fragrant wife. Maybe tonight could make things different or otherwise convince me that I had a reason to keep trying.

When George arrived at home later that evening I was dressed in his favorite ankle length black satin robe; that didn't close all the way. I had nothing underneath, just the way he liked it. The pedicure on my toes were strapped up in four inch red stiletto heels. It was evening now and George had just pulled into the garage.

I heard the car door shut as I took one last look in the mirror at my body and hair. Everything was perfect! I rushed to the door to open it for him with sunshine in my smile but George seemed irritable. In haste, he walked in the door and gave me his coat to hang up while he went straight to the dining room. No kiss, no hug, no words were spoken in the romantically ambient home; same ole' same ole'.

As I followed him to the table, I put his things down. All I could think about was what is his problem? I looked good, smelled good, my skin was exfoliated and soft, why is he always missing it? Hamilton would have wasted no time to embrace me as his wife. We might have even skipped dinner. Maybe he smelled his scent on me. I brought our plates to the dining room where he sat waiting with expectancy.

"So, how was your trip?"

"It was actually excellent!"

He was a different man that fast; fickle.

George was almost talking to himself, I only pretended to be engaged, and he noticed none of everything I worked very hard to prepare. Emotions were on boil as he progressed through the dialogue of his manic ego.

"So what else went on during the trip?"

George stood up and got defensive.

"What do you mean what else happened on the trip?"

"George, it was just a question."

"There you go, always accusing me of something."

"What are you talking about?"

"You know exactly what I'm talking about."

Abruptly, George got up from the table and went into the kitchen, pulled out a bottle of apple juice from the refrigerator, tipped the jug up in the air and drank the juice right out of the container. I couldn't believe my eyes, who is this man? My George knew I hated that.

"See Nicky, this is the kind of stuff that makes me want to leave."

"You've got to be kidding me! Ha! It's all about you George, isn't it?"

"Well, I am the head of this house, aren't I?"

"You know what . . . "

"What? What are you going to do? Where are you going to go?"

"Wow, George. Really? What's gotten into you?

"It's time you get it in your head that I run this house. You would be nothing without me."

He's clearly delusional, I thought.

"You really believe that, huh?"

"I go on these trips and there are plenty of women doing the same thing I do, at my level, teaching, caring about other people. Then I come home to you, needy and wanting attention."

"So the truth comes out!"

I pulled the pins from my hair. It was going to be a night like so many others; more arguments and nothing different.

"Why not?"

The elephant in the room was running ramped through the house; he was no longer a secret. I was kind of glad.

"You think you're the only one bored in this relationship? All I do is cater to you, clean the house, cook, laundry, listen to all of your stories, give, give, give and all you do is take, take, take, how boring is that! I'm bored out of my mind!"

"How could you possibly be bored? Besides I thought you liked doing all that stuff. You sure fooled me."

"Of course you'd say that. You're too wrapped up in yourself to see anything outside of you, including knowing what I like."

"You're the one who is supposed to know what you like, that's the problem!"

"You might be right about that . . . "

"I knew what I wanted from you ever since day one. You were beautiful, feisty; I could only imagine how good you were in bed. I wanted that, I wanted you, why? Because that's what I like!"

I didn't know whether to cry or to stab his hand with a fork. He basically just told me all I was was a good lay he could keep at his house. I have to admit, that hurt. I had been trying hard to love him, my efforts both exhausted and unnoticed left me perplexed on whether I should leave or go. I didn't know what I wanted to do next, but not him. He knew and was still talking.

" . . . then, there you go talking all that love stuff, so I figured it couldn't be too bad, you were fine as hell, what could be worse than that?

"HA! Plenty, like being married to you!"

How dare he disrespect me like that? Hamilton would never speak to me in such disrespect. His offer of love rang in my ear as I washed the dinner dishes like a mad woman.

"Don't play yourself George! You may have only wanted to sleep with me, but how do you know the feeling wasn't mutual? You actually don't even know who you are married to! I became a wife, I wasn't always one. And you know good and well you were the one who fell in love first! So . . . "

George laughs.

"Now see, that's what I like; feisty."

I shook my head drying the plates.

"And you're right, babe. I did fall in love with you first. I just wanted to see how you would respond to what I was saying. Just starting a little trouble. "

"Why would you do that?"

George walked up behind me at the sink and pressed his groin against my backside.

"Cause I miss the way things used to be. Besides, you know how I get when I travel, I missed you, baby."

"Yea, I guess. I worked hard to make things perfect for when you got home, so that maybe things could be different between us. We argue all the time and I'm tired of it."

"I understand and I commend your efforts."

Repulsed by the way George felt up my body; every place he touched seemed to sting like a bee's prick. The dishes were already dry, but I kept drying them to keep from breaking down crying.

"Shouldn't marriage be different? I mean shouldn't we at least get along?"

I turned around to face my husband, George. Standing face to face and in unison we agreed for the first time ever,

"Yes, it should be different." We said in unison.

George leaned in to kiss me but I just couldn't. I walked away toward the bedroom.

"Why'd you do that?"

"Because George, it's going to take more than that . . . "

"What do you mean, Nicky? That's proof right there that we are on the same page . . . "

"No its not George, and even still, at this point, it's not enough."

"Oh, now it's not enough?"

"No, not anymore. And see there you go

again. Instead of leading us to a place of solution, you only lead yourself into being concerned with just you. You don't ever take into consideration how I might feel or what might make me happy . . . "

"You are crazy, woman! Don't I provide this house for you? What about the nice cars in our drive way? Don't you always have your hair done and are sent to spa's and out to eat, all that! Isn't that enough? What more could you possibly want?"

"Love."

"Love?"

"I want to share my soul with you, George. I want to be intimately a part of the fabric that makes up the person you are. I want our love to soar into the heavens, and be heaven on earth."

"What are you talking about? What do clothes have to do with this?' Here's how I see it, we have plenty of sex! I don't get it. I thought we were already doing all this stiff you're talking about.. I swear you are one ungrateful . . . "

"Oh don't you dare!"

"Well I'm just saying."

"That's my point, don't even go there! You know what? I'm done."

George was right, what if he had already given me the depth of his shallow soul? It obviously wasn't enough for me. But if it was the best he had to offer me, do I settle or compromise? After all he was my husband.

George followed behind me as I went to bed. There were no words spoken the rest of the night as we lay in the bed together; separately. George moved as close as he could until he was inside of me. I was too tired to fight, he missed the bus, boat and the train; he didn't get it and I couldn't make him. After last night, the distance between the love I desired and the affection he wanted was a light years difference from what Hamilton and I shared. Once George was asleep I turned on my nightstand light and wrote in between his snores.

Nicky's Journal Entry

Love Be Gone

If I left you, would you be blue?
Would you feel sad if I didn't turn to you?
If I let my soul slip into yours, would you welcome me? Would you reject the notion and put a spell on me?

If I left you, what would you do?
Would it be too late to finally come thru?
Would it be our fate to accept the truth?
Would you humble yourself to prove your, "I love you?"

Or would it finally be the end
...of me and you?

Nicky

Compromised
CHAPTER 6

Water runs down my back. I close my eyes and remember the last image I had of Hamilton from six months before. The memories come often and like a flood to which I only swim upstream. There was little privacy toweling dry at the gym. For the first time in a long time, George slept in. So I left to workout.

In the locker room a group of women were talking about their husbands. Not one woman had anything good to say about their man. One woman even bragged about her finding out that her husband of the twenty-six years had been cheating on her for at least twenty-three of them and although he didn't know it, she's got her revenge ten times over. Actually she was headed to meet straight from the gym. She couldn't wait for him to bend her over the family pool table. That's when I checked out. There is no way in this world that I would lie down and accept that type of ridiculous behavior in *my* relationship. Why be married? Why didn't she just tell her husband she knew when the first indiscretion happened? What's with the detrimental payback?

Glancing at the woman in disgust; I could see myself. Maybe all of us do that. Obviously they both are searching for something that they can't find in each other. So then why be together then? Is that really a "marriage?" Questions filled the brim of my minds capacity; my cup overflowed as I thought about how I was doing the same thing. Why am I wasting my life with George? What am I looking for? And why am I still feeling like I don't have it?

Although the emotional connection was seared, we continued to look the part for all of the people watching in our community, our church, and our neighbors.

Six months had passed since our last argument with each other. But the argument within of do I stay or go churned like curdled milk, well over six months. After my time with Hamilton, I knew I had to leave. It was now a matter of when and how do I say it. I needed to figure out a nice way to tell George that I didn't want to be married to him anymore. I don't know why it felt so hard to do, it was easier with Hamilton; guilt made things so much easier. Somehow the torment of this relationship was constricting and I needed to break free of the shackles. I had to tell him today.

Anticipation lifted with the garage door when I arrived home. It was definitely going to be an argument I was ready for. His car was gone, phew! I have more time. Entering the house was like no other time before. I didn't even look to see what I was doing; shoes off by the door, keys on the counter, purse on the moon table behind the couch. When my purse fell on the floor I looked up to see the house was completely empty.

Frantically I called George.

"Hello?"

"George, we've been robbed!"

George didn't respond.

"George? Are you there? Did you hear me? Someone robbed us! Where are you?"

A women's voice in the background came through the phone crystal clear.

"Wait, who is that?"

"Nicky, you know we have been having problems for some time now . . . "

I hung up the phone. I was supposed to be the one get rid of him first. Karma weaseled her way in again, I hate her!

George continued to call back, I hit ignore three times. When he called the fourth time, I answered.

"What, George?"

"The bottom line is this, I have moved out and I'm done with you."

"Done, with me? Like I'm some used toy?

"You're right Nicky, I'm done with us."

The woman in the background told him to say that.

"I just don't want to pretend anymore. We haven't been in love in a long time, if ever. It's time to stop playing with love. Life is too short to do anything else!"

"Are you kidding me? So, all of this time you've been cheating on me, George?"

"Not really . . . "

"What? How do you "not really" cheat on your wife?"

My senses kicked in and I knew exactly how as I remembered the smell Hamilton all over my body. He was nowhere around, but all around me inside of my empty home. Thoughts of him recalled feeling of what it felt like to be wrapped in his arms leaned up against my car, just some months back. It was then that I realized I was much more familiar with "not really" possibilities than I accused George of.

"It's kind of a long story, but I have loved this woman since we were children. She is the mother of my only child and it's time we stopped fighting our feelings and just live out what is destiny; our love with our family."

"I thought your daughter's mother had died?"

"She almost did. My daughter and I have been taking care of her since she got out of the hospital."

My thoughts and words were lost in the sincerity of his loving gesture. Had this really all come full circle? Betrayed, hurt and alone all over again. And to think it was just one bad decision that got me where I am today, engulfed in turmoil wishing I could pull back the hands of time and decide differently, decide to stay with what was my destiny; Hamilton's love.

"Are you there, Nicky?"

"Yes I'm here."

By now I had made my way into what was our bedroom. My closet was already packed, boxes were stacked spilling out from the walk in closet and into the bedroom. He was serious. Everything was so organized and neat, like a woman did it. Like he had planned this for months, maybe even years. If he was half as serious about our relationship as he was about packing my things, then maybe we could have worked it out; we could have changed destiny, right?

"You don't have anything to say? I really never meant to hurt you."

"You know what, George?"

"What, Nicky?"

He was convincingly peaceful in his tone, like he was caught up in the rapture of love, for real.

"I hope you and your true love enjoy the rest of your lives in the bliss and harmony we never got to experience."

"Thank you, Nicky. That was really big of you to say."

"It's fine George. I mean it, besides I'm too tired for any drama."

"I appreciate that. Well listen, I have movers ready to move your belongings wherever you need them to go. You'll have three days to let me know and then the offer is no longer available."

"How considerate, George."

Sarcasm dripped from my heart; half stone, half flesh.

"No problem!"

As usual, George didn't pick up on the sarcasm. Nor was he aware that, I had been saving my allowance money for a rainy day. I guess I always knew we wouldn't be together; he didn't mention any missing money, so I neither did I. I hung up the phone and that was the end of me and George.

Where am I going? I had no friends, no sister, no husband or child to hold. Just me, what do I do with that?

In the house, a vacant "empty nest," I walked the walls, running my fingers along the once colorful walls that were full of life. Now they were blank and white; like no one had ever lived there before. I thought about all the things I used to want our home to be filled with like, love, warmth and trust. There was only one place on this earth like that besides Hamilton's heart; my grandmother's house deep in the woods of Savannah. I called my grandmother who welcomed the idea of a visit with open arms.

I've heard a lot of people say that their grandmother was "something else." Not my grandma. My grandmother was something special. I knew that if there really was a God who loved like she said, I had no doubt he was her friend. He loved her and showed it daily. She was a beautiful eighty year old woman with caramel tight skin with long light gray colored hair.

Grandma lived alone in a modest house with fields all around. There was a huge oak tree that sat in the front yard for years. I used to swing on its branches as a little girl. I couldn't wait to embrace the peace that lived in the air in and around her house. I also couldn't wait to hug my grandma. I needed a good hug from her.

As I pulled into the long driveway the dust

of red dirt made my arrival nothing short of a sandy entrance. I tipped the cab and walked toward the porch. Grandma was sitting in her chair, waiting for me. She was older looking than I'd last seen her, but more beautiful than she's ever been. Granddaddy's chair was still next to hers on the porch. He was her Hamilton; her one true love. He passed away of a stroke exactly one year before my wedding with Hamilton. As soon as I hugged her warm, round body, tears began to fall. We sat on the steps for a while and I cried in her arms, like my heart just flat lined. She held me and didn't say a word.

On most days grandma left me alone. A sweet and wise woman, But whenever she did insert herself to speak, things seemed to change. Like a wizard's magic wand, she had power; her friend never seemed to let her down.

I spent many days with grandma, sometimes doing nothing at all. It was quiet. She had no TV and a car she only took to the grocery store and church, she loved her simple country life. We went to church every Sunday, something I hadn't done since I lived there as a little girl. It was good. I could see over the table now, so I understood a lot more of what the preacher was trying to say. Grandma's house on Sunday after church grandma was like eating at a buffet. She cooked big meals, enough to feed the whole town, and they all came. I cleaned up after dinner and she routinely went to bed, while the night was still young. Monday's were the best days there. After I stopped crying all the time, I was angry and went walking often through the large grasslands to yell at the trees and write my poetry; a recipe for healing. It always felt better that way.

Divorce papers from George finally arrived in the mail. I rocked in granddaddy's rocking chain on the front porch. I was expecting them but holding the papers in hand made for an agonizing reflection of all my relationship failures. I swear the sky was falling, the clouds seemed heavy, flattened me to the ground; I was crushed.

"Nicky!" Grandma yelled from the kitchen.

"Yes, Grandma?"

I heard Grandma's voice from the front porch. Holding the divorce papers tightly in hand, I ran to the kitchen from the porch. When I got there, grandma was humming. She stopped when I entered.

"Baby, can you pass me that sugar, there?"

I put the papers on the table and handed her the big bag of sugar that was in arms reach away from her.

"Thank you, baby."

"You're welcome, grandma."

I turned to walk out of the kitchen back to the quiet porch to sulk over my divorce papers.

"One more thing before you go, sweetheart."

"Sure grandma, what do you need?"

"Have a seat, darling. I wanna talk to you for a minute."

In the seven weeks that I had been there, grandma didn't say much of anything so nervousness came over me, like the days when I used to get in trouble as a little girl. I had seen many spankings in that kitchen. I felt like I was about to get another one; the one I deserved, the kind where its twinge makes its way into your soul.

"Listen, baby many people are tricked by the devil because they only look for him to come in a red suit, wearing horns on his head and a pitchfork in his hand. But that ain't the way he comes. Not always. He'll trick you good, he's deceitfully cunning. He's even sexy." She paused to laugh.

"Baby, he's very clever, and that's why you miss him so much. Other times folks give him way too much credit. Pass me that there salt?"

She knew she had my full attention.

"Here, grandma."

"Thank you, Suga."

She didn't miss a beat.

"You see, baby, only God knows the difference between what's good for you and what's not. The only way for you to figure it out is if you get close enough to Him to hear him tell you what that difference is. You understand what I say, child?"

"Yes ma'am, I do."

"Alright baby."

I walked out of the kitchen slowly, she didn't say it but it was time for me to go. Her words felt right, although it ripped open my soul and exposed the tender nature of my whole heart, now all flesh. It was raining outside, beating heavy on the front porch, like wolves banging, taunting me to come out in the rain. A jolt of thunderous fear struck me, rattling my bones forcing me to run, far away from what I felt.

I ran as fast as I could through the door, into the rain until I entered the safety of the covered wooded area. There was no difference between my tears and the gray clouds releasing above me; the sky cried in solace with me. Thunder shook the ground beneath me, I buckled to my knees in fear, face wet and filled with tears. Anger erupted from my soul. The thunder and I yell at the trees in harmony.

"You tricked me again, I fell straight in, damn you Nicky! You gave in to sin. All it took was a "Hello ma'am," messed up your whole flow. It messed up your rhythm girl and rocked you to the core because you were so pressed to sell your soul for love.

On my knees my soul bellowed out and I cried.

Hurt and despair now far beyond repair and restless in its stare laughing at me as I stand alone in these woods, away from it all still holding the phone absent of a receiver who made me a believer till I was tricked by the deceiver, of love.

How could I be so stupid!

Now there's no one to tell, no one to turn to, no one to understand all that I've been through.

I pleaded for change and only hoped someone would hear me. Maybe grandma's friend would listen in and save me from me.

God, if you are listening, please break these chains; take these chains far away from me, and set me free! Release me from the stain of guilt that responded to the sound of evil teasing my heart with what I don't know love to be. Show me your way and your light, guide me please. I'm tired of this fight; I just don't have it in me anymore."

I waited for a response and heard nothing. However, I did feel something. I could feel something powerfully divine was near. Then the thunder stopped and the rain turned to drizzle. I couldn't abandon the truth any longer; it revealed itself. It chased me and wrestled with me in my grandmother's field until it broke me; I was broken by the search for love. I fought for its preeminence in my life a long time and had sold myself short to experience just a glimpse of its strength.

But in this final fight, I felt my soul had won. I had overcome and the fight for love was finished. For the first time ever I decided to love me enough to let love find me. I wasn't going to chase it anymore. It would come to me when it was supposed to and I was going to let it.

Coming out of the thick of the cooling comfort of the trees, I could see the sun. I stepped into its light, free, and completely renewed and walked slowly toward grandma rocking on the porch. She didn't say a word, just smiled. We both knew that it was time for me to go back. I kissed her sweet soft cheek.

"Thank you, grandma."

"You're welcome, baby."

I went to my room and packed my things. The cab wouldn't be here for another hour, so I decided to write something quickly. I had to mark this moment of freedom with a journal entry. I was different, alive again; uncompromising, evenly tempered, "Evenly yoked."

A new start in an old city was exactly what I needed; I couldn't wait to get back home.

Nicky's Journal Entry

Sunrise

Entrenched in the water I found a pocket of hope. I can breathe again. Baptized in mystery only belief can hear. I feel a piece of me again.

Kissed by the breeze that illuminated my thirst
Warm is my belly, sunshine I birthed.

Removal of fake beauty returned the unfading loveliness of inner self. I pledged to take care of her in sickness to full health.

Effective was the wind that tossed me to and fro.
Long and strong it shook me until I awoke to enjoy the sunrise. Now, I have arrived.

My being is present.
My joy is restored and my soul is evident as I humbly accept the gift of a new day, God's way.

"Evenly Yoked"

The Encounter
CHAPTER 7

It's Saturday morning and I'm all moved in to my new place. The trip back was long, but being settled made it worth.

I knew I needed to avoid the idle time of disaster; no more itching. So I can't sleep in; the bookstore is where I shall go; a different one, disconnected from anything familiar. I don't want to let go of this spiritual ecstasy I feel, I've never felt it; a euphoric encounter, like I experienced at my grandmother's house, a bottled moment of climax, release, and freedom. It was a beautiful day, walking to the book store seemed to fit a new beginning, so I walked.

Imprisoned by growths endless bounds, the more I fantasized about what I wanted, the more I was hesitant to the idea of having a different experience. I froze in front of the book store for a split second until the customer behind me forced me to have to go in.

In the book store I thought I heard a familiar voice but I couldn't see over the crowd surrounding the author who was sitting down and looked to be signing books. The fans just about blocked the door way. As I moved closer into the store I saw a poster that read "Meet Author Hamilton Wright . . . " My heart started pounding, everyone started to look at me like they could hear it; they parted like the red sea and I had full view of him, it really was him; destiny.

"Hamilton?"

He looked up and smiled hugely. We laughed.

"I don't believe it." I said aloud.

Hamilton was older, mature and more handsome than I'd ever seen him before. He glowed with greatness. I stood in awe of him. Something was noticeably different.

I stood in line anxiously waiting to greet him properly. The line moved as slow as molasses. One step, one customer, felt like eternity. I wanted to knock the line down like bowling pins, until it was me next in line. I was so proud of the man he had become, we were older now, but he seemed to have let nothing get in his way, not love, not me, not anything. I couldn't believe my eyes. Not because I was in disbelief of his ability, he had always been a smart man. I couldn't believe that I was going to see him again. Maybe we would even touch again, I only hoped. His touch always electrocuted my mind, body, and soul; blew my fuse. He was a constant in making me feel alive, I knew I did the same for him; some kind of irresistible we were. Was this loves way of finding me? Was Hamilton my destiny?

Finally it was my turn. Hamilton was excitedly surprised to see me and it showed.

"I can't believe that it's really you."

Hamilton stood up and hugged me so tightly, my feet lifted from up off of the ground. I closed my eyes for that brief moment of embrace, home again, at last. As my feet touched the ground again, reality continued.

"What a surprise to see you!"

"Yes, likewise." I said safely.

It would be just my luck if he was married.

"I just moved to this area, do you come here often?"

He nodded his head but was busy signing my book. I couldn't read any of the words upside down. Hamilton finished signing the book and handed it back to me.

"Well, I appreciate your support and hopefully we'll meet again."

"Ok, sounds good."

Was that it? The crowd shoved me back to the door. Holding the door open I turned around and watched Hamilton as he signed more books and took pictures with the book buyers. I closed the door; that was it.

I walked past my apartment, the book clinched in my hand. I couldn't put a finger on what I felt so I kept walking and ended up at the park in midtown. I found a bench to sit on by myself and placed the book and my bag on either side of me, to people watch.

I sat watching dog walkers, roller bladders and runner's pass by. People were busy, not thinking about love; why was I? A Frisbee hit my head and as I turned around to see who'd done it, my things fell to the ground. I grabbed my bag, and reached for my book which was open to the page Hamilton had signed.

Nicky, I see you are ring-less these days. . . You have always been the one true love of my life. I don't know what happened, but I'm sure glad to see you, and must see you again. I need more time with you while I'm in town, and who knows maybe take you away with me, forever! What else can two single people do in this situation? Call me around 5 pm at 555-777-9987. I need to see you again. . .and this time I'm not letting you go!

Love, Hammy

It was destiny! Love had found me this time. I was sure of it. I grabbed my bag and held the book in my hand and ran all the way back to my apartment, it was 4:45pm. I was at least a mile and a half away. I ran as fast as I could, smiling the entire way; bumping a few people along the way.

"Sorry sir, excuse me!"

A few choice words and some hand gestures weren't going to stop me, not today. I didn't care. I couldn't. I had an appointment. My fourth chance at love had arrived, and I wasn't going to miss it.

Maybe this was the decision I should have made the first time; stick with my husband. Or maybe this was the way it was supposed to be, so I could appreciate my husband. Our differences and the challenges never faded the light our love shines.

Suddenly, I had a though that stopped me dead in my tracks. What if he didn't like the new me? I was out of breath and only one block away from my apartment, what if the new me wasn't his destiny? I walked slowly for the last meter of the race; my watch said 4:55. Or maybe, this was our chance to experience the ecstasy I had been longing to experience with a God who rescued me from drowning in my thirst for love; and my destiny, my man Mr. Hamilton Wright. Is this moment finally here? My feet started to quicken, then moved faster and a little faster until my pace restored to full speed until I reached my apartment and caught the first elevator going up.

As I waited for the slow elevator to get on my floor, all I could think about was that I made it.! I turned the key to my apartment door at 4:58 pm, with two minutes to spare. I threw the keys on the counter, dug through my bag for my phone, whipped out the book to get the number only to realize my phone was dead. Uggh! Are you kidding me! Why is there something always in my way!

It's 5:01 pm. I hurried to find my charger and jammed it into the wall so the phone could charge up to at least one bar. Anticipation had the best of me. Every minute felt like an eternity! I was so excited about the possibility of sharing our love with each other forever, the way it was supposed to be.

By 5:05pm I had one bar. That was good enough to rip the phone from the charger in the wall and call him.

"Hello?"

"Hamilton?

"Yes . . . "

"Its Nicky."

"I know . . . "

I could feel his smile over the phone and it warmed my ear; he didn't need to say anything else. We stayed on the phone for one hour before Hamilton actually invited me out for dinner. There was so much to talk about; neither one of us wanted to hang up even though we knew we'd see each other soon.

"I love you."

"I love you too, Hammy"

I was slow to end the call. There was something about hanging up that I just didn't want to do.

"Nicky!"

"Yes, Hammy?"

"Don't leave me this time."

I knew I had to be careful with my response. He was giving me his whole heart for the second time.

"I won't, Hamilton."

"Just you and I this time, right?"

"Yes, baby. Just you and me; destiny, right?"

"Right!"

He sound happily relieved; he needed the reassurance. This time, I knew how to give it. We ended the call and I immediately undressed to get in the shower. I took my time in the shower and getting dressed. I had to be sure to look amazing.

Staring in the mirror at myself in the mirror and thinking about all of the things I had been through I admired that I still looked good, real good! I had smile lines around my mouth, crow's feet around my eyes and a silver streak in the front of my hair; but I was beautiful. I realized God brought me here. O better yet, he brought love to me. I guess he was my friend now too. A tear rolled down my face and smudged my make-up. I didn't care, I couldn't. So I just closed my eyes, took a deep slow breath, and finally, soulgasmed.

There were no words for this moment. There was only room for the silent embrace of each breath taken. I breathed heavily in excitement. I was finally ready to take on the risk of love with a genuine thankfulness for the journey's new beginning.

Taking a deep breath I fixed my makeup just in time for the knock at the door. It was Hamilton. In the doorway of my apartment, we kissed, incredibly, emotionally, spiritually tied together. Love seemed to have found us both. Until I woke up to a knock at the door.

"Nicky, it's me, are you awake?" He said.

I laid still in my bed. Hoping, wishing, praying that he would just go away if I didn't let him know I was there. Maybe he'd think he had the wrong room if I didn't move, not even to breathe.

"Nicky, I just want to talk for a minute. Please open the door?"

He knew I was there. I walked over to the door. The closer I got to it, the more I could feel his energy; pulling me in. I stood behind the door with my back up against it vulnerable and he kept knocking, begging me to open it. I didn't know what made me feel more nervous, the vibration of the knock or the sound of his voice. They both made my legs weak. I could hardly stand up.

"Go away Terrance." I mouthed to myself.

Is this nightmare really coming true? I can't believe he's really here. My soon to be husband is down the hall, what is he thinking!

"Nicky, we need to talk. I want to talk to you."

I didn't say a word. There wasn't anything to say. Especially after what I just dreamed, it felt so real. And right now, I can't believe the mess I dreamt was really standing on the other side of my destination wedding cruise room door.

"Nicky, let me in. It's cold out here."

"That's not my problem." I said firmly. But I couldn't walk away from the door. I needed to hear him walk away so I could breathe. But he didn't move.

"Nicky, I promise we will just talk."

"You promise?"

"Yes, I promise."

With his promise, I opened the door.

Part 3

Soulgasm

A NOTE FROM THE AUTHOR

The Soul

THE DIMENSIONAL YOU

How many people do you know that actually live their life under the assumption that an inner core or inner self exists? More likely than not, you probably do not know many; the downward spiral of reciprocity for humanity and the erosion of identity among other societal statistics prove this to be true. As creatures of habit influenced by the cultural temperature of a sexually driven environment assumes that there is a sense of unawareness toward an inner self that has developed and matured against the ideologies of purity, unity, intellectuality and divine likeness. All of which are conduits for change. You see, there is something to be said about the process of change, where it begins, and what it's influenced by; the inner self.

Over a life's span there are infinite occasions where you might feel that a piece of your inner self has gotten lost in the shuffle of experiences, dissipated from experiences or has even seemed to have completely disappear to where you either don't know who you are or have become something so far away from where you want to be that you may have deemed yourself a lost cause. Connecting to your inner self can help to close the gaps between discovering or rediscovering the divine essence of who you are; your soul. The reason why is because, your Soul is not something you have. Your soul is something you are.

Your soul is made up of mind, body, matter and other faculties. And if it is true that your mind and body are inseparable faculties of your soul, to only think of yourself as having a soul, believes that you are in need of something you already are. Have you allowed your mind to believe in the anticipation of needing a soul instead of accepting the limitless potential of being the beautiful soul that you already are? This is easier to do than you may think, especially for women. Life circumstances can present themselves with such an intense amount of pressure that the birthing of any dream, hope, or fantasy is left crushed or exposed; creating a feeling of spiritually vulnerable nudity. This feeling of nakedness produces an opening or an access to the depth of your soul therefore allowing the light of truth to illuminate your precise intentions; good or otherwise, leaving you then, with a choice. The decision you must make in that moment of pivotal revelation is how you decide to live out the rest of your life from that moment forward.

In your decision, you have two choices. You can decide to either use the issues being exposed as an opportunity to embrace the footloose fancy freedom of your soul's journey; therefore accepting the responsibility of any mistakes, mishaps or poor choices to see them as an exploration that has allowed you to grow and awaken the potential that God has woven into the very DNA of your being. Or you can believe that you need to suffocate, drown in or hide the issues that come to light. Women are the masters of cover up; we know how to make cover up look really good; flawless. However, cover up can also cover up the beauteous liberty held in the power of you individual womanhood. So then and to this point, which option have you decided to live *your* life by?

As a woman, it is within a fundamentally intuitive, nurture-like nature that the latter is chosen. Many women tend to swaddle their issues in pretty blankets, laced in comfort-ability; without even realizing the issues they have so carefully and skillfully cloaked to ignore, have been wrapped in a way that always leaves the truth exposed. The truth is evident in the world around you with women misplaced in the order of life, in women emasculating men, in women tearing one another down and not supporting each in growth, in divorce rates, in a lack corporate and religious ethics, and the list continues, but as the Chinese proverb states,

"If there is beauty in the soul
there will be beauty in the person.
If there is beauty in the person,
there will be harmony in the house.
If there is harmony in the house,
there will order in the nation.
If there is order in the nation,
there will be peace in the world."

As God would design it, women are born to contribute to the growth, nurturing and protecting others, not the hiding of the same. Unfortunate to its gender, not enough women remove their cover up or in other words apply their "motherly instinct," toward soul choices of whom or what is allowed to enter in their space. In turn an overexposed soul dies from self-destruction. What about you? Are you on the verge of self destruction? You don't have to be. Just like Nicky, it's never too late to make the choice for your soul to LIVE!

The foundation of a woman's soul is built upon the innate genius of being a preserver and birthing agent of life. However if you have allowed your circumstances to disable your capacity to exhaust your soul's natural instinct, you have intrinsically denied your being, your personality, your soul its righteous responsibility to live in the intent of your purpose as well as in the order of life.

This is why the delicacy of a woman's soul must seek to be extremely careful not to neglect itself from living as the unlimited being she was divinely created to be. And if you find success in taping into your soul's circumference you can perpetually avoid three spiritually destructive ploys that present itself in a woman's life: an abort, a miscarriage, or a premature delivery.

In the light of biblical understanding, the meaningful depth of a woman's soul is fulfilled; conversely there is also a scientific explanation of the soul to be gleaned in order to holistically understand the spiritual apt of a woman's soul.

The systemic perspective of the soul is based on a scientific theory called Superstrings Physics; presented by Pete Sanders. The scientific explanation of the soul otherwise known as Superstring Physics is based upon the theory that the soul's elements all tie together as it travels through the universe of space and time.

According to physics the soul is divided up into Protons (matter), Electrons (energy), photons (light), and gravitons (mysterious force that makes gravity). Top physicists agree that the strings exist in a minimum of ten dimensions (three of space, one of time and six others they don't have the technology to measure). According to Pete Sanders, scientists can also agree that the soul is not existent on its own. Furthermore some radical scientists identify the soul as an immaterial substance made in the image of God. Assuming this theory or theories to be true, perhaps the immeasurable immaterial dimensions that science currently does not have the technology to exasperate are actually an intentional orchestration of God's divine nature. Possibly, even the truest discovery in unveiling the mysterious yet sovereign blueprint of the soul's existence, is exclusively and completely found in building a relationship with the Creator. Consider that it may be through the formation of a relationship with God that a person understands themselves and is able to communicate the difference between the strength of their soul and the power of their spirit. Therefore while your soul is inevitably who you are; which is the psyche part of your make-up to which you are able to understand yourself, connect to, and relate with people, your spirit on the other hand, can be viewed as how you connect to and relate to God. For that reason what and who you are, is a person who is a soul that has a spirit[1].

There is something to be gleaned from everything you are faced with; whether the benefit is for your soul or for your spirit,

---

[1] For the word of God is alive and active. Sharper than any double-edged sword, it penetrates even to dividing soul and spirit, joints and marrow; it judges the thoughts and attitudes of the heart. Hebrew 4:12

one or both will be impacted. The impact imposed is most determined by what you choose to surround yourself with. As you traverse through life your spiritual survival and the operation of living out its divine power in the natural realm is vastly dependent upon understanding the difference between your connection to God and your connection with self.

No matter the depth of your soul's intent or reasoning nothing can be hidden from God. He is omnisciently omnipresent; knowing about everything about everyone, everywhere. Even when you may be unaware of His presence, He *is* there. You have no secrets from God, and even still, guess what? He loves you. He knows your soul and understands your spirit because you are connected.

Relationship with your Creator is powerful enough to penetrate the core of your moral and spiritual life no matter how crazy it may be or has been. This means that at any point in your life, you can reach out and connect with him. Your relationship with God is built upon a discernment of what is within, both good and evil. Under the Christian belief it is also a key element as to why you must be born again of spirit; a rebirth of your connection to God.

"Jesus answered, "Very truly I tell you, no one can enter

the kingdom of God unless they are born of water and the Spirit.
Flesh gives birth to flesh, but the Spirit gives birth to spirit." John 3: 5-6

The background of this particular verse of scripture is referring to Jesus and his travels to Jerusalem for Passover. Most Jews in that day did their best to avoid the region of Samaria in their travels due to differences of what the Jews thought to be righteous customs and culture, however it was the shortest route to Jerusalem; so, Jesus went. He ended up in Samaria, cleared the temple and spent some time talking with Nicodemus who was a prominent religious leader at the time; he was there talking to him about eternal life. In their discussion Jesus explained to him the importance of a spiritual rebirth, saying that people will not enter the Kingdom (heaven) by the exclusion of living a better life, but rather by the inclusion of being spiritually reborn. He further made sure to declare the consequential benefits of living the balance between soul and spirit. The fine line of how to live in balance harmoniously between soul and spirit is possible through the act of soul preservation.

SOUL PRESERVATION

Some women are entrapped by the idea of love to the point that they miss the meaning within the principle of love. Confusion of this co[illegible]ips or material things whose only mask is lust. Such relationships do not end until the woman has slept with the enemy unprotected, unpreserved and their soul is scarred and pregnant with disaster.

Soul preservation is all about protecting the intimate connect point of your soul to others. Moreover, soul preservation has everything to do with keeping your soul and spirit safe within the context of your environment; whether you can change that environment or not. One thing you to remember is that even blood sucking mosquitoes are drawn to the warmth and brightness of the light. Therefore it is imperative to cautiously preserve and protect the light, God's light that resonates through you. Why, because as a human being you innately desire intimacy; whether it's a mosquito or not. This human longing for intimacy is the bridge that can open and close the access to toxic and healthy relationships.

> "Intimacy involves making our innermost experience at least partially accessible to others, and to have these experiences validated by the others. How partners respond to each other's fears and needs, and the manner in which thoughts and feelings are exchanged . . . strongly influences the state of the relationship." (Greenberg & Matau, Marques, 1998)

In translation this means that when you carry the baggage of hurt, pain, and betrayal it can leave the heart of your soul full with no room to cherish the purposeful and progressive identificatio

Whether you realize it or not, God's love is the elect speech to which life is expressed. Without pretending, His love preserves an immeasurable sufficiency of the soul's needs and then through human nature makes the ability of its effect and display intimately divine. While God's divine love is immeasurable, the intimacy of how you connect to God's love or give this love to others cannot be given without measure. In rationed portions you may want to consider how the level of your soul's intimacy is dispersed within the day by day protection of the relationships connected to your soul. It might be time to kill a few mosquitoes, before they suck the life out of you! This will help you to avoid a dream abortion, a miscarriage of destiny, a premature delivery of purpose or the internal confrontation with the emptiness left within your soul's faculties.

SOUL FACULTIES

Adapted by Aristotle's theory of the soul, there are three primary faculties of the soul to highlight; nutrition, sensation, and movement. When any of these three primary faculties go unfulfilled or are left vulnerable, you have created a spiritual gateway for temptation, lust, addictions and abusive or self destructive behavior. These symptoms can unlock the deviant nature of [illegible] f your spirits ability to connect with your Creator and excel beyond what may be negative circumstances.

With the faculty of nutrition people get to live out the cliché, “You are what you eat.” Let’s pause for a moment and think about that. What are you fueling your body with? Are they mostly healthy? Are they mostly sweet? Are they mostly chocolate? More specifically, how does your body feel after you consume whatever it is you are eating? When you have poor eating habits, your body not only knows it, it shows it! It shows it in a loss of focus, in forms of depression, or event a loss of figure; muffin top jeans. Adversely it can also show up in the opposite extremity to where a woman is so afraid to eat that she forces herself to vomit not allowing her own body to break down the nutrients from the waste. Unfortunately if you do not take care to consider your nutrition in the same extreme you can get so thin, that everyone will be able to see your entire bone frame; for example with extreme anorexia. Medical statistics prove there to be a strong correlation between poor eating habits and mental and physical diseases. A disease is some type of “dis-ease” to the body causing a breakdown and opening. But you can close this opening by way of thinking about what you eat. While your diet may not be the only cause to being receptive to or to be contracted with disease, statistics do prove that nutriti f you are in a dangerous place with your health, find a personal trainer, nutritionist, and/or therapist and get back on track-your soul is depending upon it!

As women who are purposed to carry destiny you may also want to consider your spiritual nutrition. Spiritual nutrition considers similar questions. Pause for a moment and think about the things you fuel your spirit with. Is it healthy? Is it heavy in toxic relationships? Is heavy in sexuality? How does your soul feel after each encounter? When you have poor spiritual habits, your soul will crave the nutrition that it is lacking from any and everything that may have a close resemblance. As a result you can become clingy. Furthermore, if you only fill your soul with "junk food" or if you don't feed your soul enough nutrients you have successfully deprived your soul the proper nutrition needed to live and function within all its faculties in the natural and spiritual realm. At which point you are open play because your strength is lost in the lack of soulful nutrition.

With the faculty of sensation it allows you to feel aware as a woman. The sensation faculty carries a emotionally cognitive stem. This is the faculty that allows you to have thoughts, beliefs, and reasoning; whether they are true or false. Sensation is the faculty that opens you up to feeling some kind of way about

Have you ever had a bad dream that felt so real that you were mad at your friend or spouse after you woke up? If you have, then you experienced the sensationalism of the sensation faculty of your soul. Conversely this means that the faculty of sensation has the power to awaken an awareness that can also open up your emotions.

Women rather than men are usually more in tune with how they feel. Emotions are the things you feel, but they are not what you believe. Flowing in this vein, the soul faculty of sensation carries a "super" power of feeling some may refer to as intuition. Imagine yourself at the last social event you attended. Maybe you were with your girlfriends just hanging out at a networking event or social gathering. Picture the room filled with new people to meet. Liken to this event, think about an experience you had when you met a particular person for the first time. Beyond what you thought about that person, what could you feel? Did if feel "right?" Or was there something just not right about them? Was it almost like something hit you in the gut and just wouldn't let go? On the flipside, maybe you felt like you instantly connected with the person. Do you remember? This is another appearance of sensation at work!

Here's a question, do you remember what you did when you got this feeling? Most women ignore it and regret such ignorance later when they have found themselves in a mess. Sound familiar? It is important to acknowledge this feeling as a message from your soul and allow your spirit to guide you to the light of truth in the situation; which may equate to a need to leave the area or disconnect from the moment. The message that your soul's faculties are sending you are for your own soul and spirits preservation. Ignore it and you've opened yourself to being a target for destruction; predators, male or female will find you. Therefore it is in your best interest not to ignore the spiritual signals or warnings when they come to you.

Concerning the faculty of movement has everything to do with getting up and moving your body, mind and soul through exercising! Did you know that a healthy active lifestyle[2] takes approximately 10,000 steps a day? An average lifestyle would be over approximately 5,000 steps. Fewer than approximately 5,000 steps are considered low activity. How many steps do you estimate to have taken today? You can never be active enough. Keep in mind, dancing also counts as steps, have some fun with your movement.

---

[2] Get Active Campaign www.letsmove.gov/get-active

R [illegible] exercise of the mind. When you read, reading things that are different expands your mind and challenges your brain to think; exercise. Consider reading something new and different in addition to your regular reading projects. If you do not consider yourself an avid reader, you've made a good start getting this far; keep up the great work! Exercising your mind can also include playing games, board games, guessing games, card games, electronic word games and so much more. Never limit the possibilities regarding the various ways your mind can be moved, to do so would be such a waste.

Exercising your spirit is about practicing spiritually enriching activities such as yoga, meditation, scripture reading and so forth. Additionally exercising of any kind requires a committed consistency, which might challenge the ideals, schedule and routine you currently flow in. You can probably find countless reasons as to why you may not be active; some of which may be valid, but the good news is that it's never too late to get active and preserve your soul. The more connected you are to your soul and all of its faculties, the more heightened your awareness, sensitivity and understanding becomes toward life, relationships and love. But when you've been hurt by a friend, a mother, a sister or a man, seeing the potential beyond the instability of emotions can be difficult.

EMOTIONAL SOUL-A-COASTER

Do you ever feel like you're going crazy sometimes? For instance one minute you may have felt that you loved a guy and the next minute, when you found out he went to lunch with another woman and didn't tell you, you felt differently, or perhaps you changed your mind because of something he said? Does that sound familiar? Is that something you find yourself doing often?

If so, you may be on the ride of your life; riding an emotional soul-a-coaster!

Some women are good at keeping tabs on how much a guy has spent on them; later misconstruing the amount of money he's spent with how much the man loves her. Other women measure a man's love by how good he makes her feel in the bedroom. Both metric systems are misrepresentations of what the emotion of love is about. Love is an emotion just as much as it is an action. Love is a decision that carries with it the responsibility of demonstrating deep care for someone or something. In other words, love is more than an emotion or something you can measure by quantities. Actually, while love serves under the sensation faculty of the soul it can also be felt in the spirit.

I n experiences a new spiritual reformation. When you allow yourself to feel and experience love on a spiritual level, you are developing a trust and dependence upon God to love you greater and more than you love yourself. Learning to seek out the unwavering love of God rather than the fickle love of mankind ultimately makes your soul more powerful enabling it the gift of love to give to others. God's love gives your love perspective and expands the capacity of love across the wings of time to protect you from being connected to a negative soul tie.

SOUL TIE

As a conduit of life and nurturer of others how can you exclude love from relationship the equation of relationships with others? Your soul was created to be connected and in relationships that flow in love. Even your spiritual relationship with God is founded upon the love He has for you. Nonetheless there are ways and reasons you might be overtaken by the detriment of any forward progression in your life because of who or what is tied to your soul.

There are various ways your soul can attach itself to someone or something. Some of the ways you have no control over. For example there is a soul tie between you and your mother or your b ... ıchangeable. However, the trick that this inevitable soul tie performs is that it can have you long for love from them even when there is no relationship present or an unhealthy relationship present. In the balance of whatever the relationship the soul tie must be counter balanced by a greater love, a deeper love; a spiritual love.

Spiritual love does not complete with others, it can't; it is the foundation to all loving things. It is within the Creator's pattern of design that we be connected; the same way plants are connected to animals that are connected to humans who are connected to God and his infinite universe. Beyond a mere connection it is the intent of the creator that harmonious living is through Godly bonds with one another. When a relationship is born where love is allowed it can flow in a healthy place of divine exchange. Therefore when you are in a relationship both parties need to come together as whole individuals that complement each other, rather than complete or compete with one another, even in a friendship. Keeping this configuration of love at the forefront of your relationship permits an evolution of growth for all parties involved. What this doesn't mean is that your husband or boyfriend or best friend won't ever get on your nerves, it just means that you each have committed to the decision of love to love and work things out despite the odds. As a counter act to your decision the perversion of the contrary will attempt to distort the loving purpose God has

Fall outs come from the internal conflict of being in the wrong position of the giving and receiving end of love. You might have experienced this before when you were in an argument that got unnecessarily out of hand all because you each had to prove your point and be right. Unless someone is able to put their own feelings aside for a moment in the moment to consider the hurt or offense of the other person, you both are rightfully in the wrong position. The exchange of humility threads the strength of love in relationships. Humility must be genuine and not phony. Pretending to be humble is a wicked manipulative tactic of seduction. Women must be careful not to use the power of seduction to manipulate love from any person, even with each other. Seduction has its place; but nowhere within the confines of manipulation a relationship to get your way.

Manipulative connections reap an ungodly impure soul tie and create a sense of abusive like authority. If you are in a controlled or manipulated relationship, get rid of it; escape swiftly, it is ungodly. Remaining in the entanglement of ungodly soul ties; sometimes difficult to break, can lead you into relationships that are negative and/or unfulfilling. And when you are unfulfilled in your relationship; having no place to deposit the love you were designed to g [illegible] ssed. And when you are not focused you can become easily distracted and when you've become easily distracted your guard gets lower and lower until it comes all the way down. And if your guard is all the way down you are open to anything and just might find yourself in unpredicted, unprotected, and compromising situations. The secret to protecting your love and letting your soul escape from the potential entanglement of a compromising situation is revealed through your spirit; connection with God.

When you think about negative soul ties, do you ever wonder why do you may have so many? Do you feel like, no matter how hard you try at relationships, you can't seem to connect to the love you want so badly to experience? And so you settle for what you can get? Do you feel like you keep creating the same pattern, with the same guys? Are you subconsciously creating chaos in your relationships and in your life?

Trust and believe you are not the only woman who thinks these thoughts. There is a way to cancel the vicious cycle of this behavior. To regain the independence of being the beautiful soul you were created you must be honest with what your vulnerability is and facing where it may have come from. When you can woman up; be honest about living out the reflection of who you are and what you stand for you can avoid becoming your own worst

Take a moment to think about where there is an entry of vulnerability in your relationships. Did you watch your mother destroy all of her relationships? Are you still hurt by the wrong doing of a previous relationship?

What is it? Is it because you are afraid to be alone? Was it the words of your parents, a child hood friend, or a rumor? What was it? Identifying your place of vulnerability is important. It exposes the wound of your soul scar (the opening) and gives you a point in time, where a soul tie was created, turned into an idol, and or created the negative waves you may be experiencing today throughout your relationship life. It might be easy for you to be able to think of one hundred situations. But you don't need one hundred situations. Each and every situation only made the wound wider and deeper, what you want to find is the opening. Let God take you to that moment of vulnerability; the root. Let Him take you there so you can detach from the ungodly soul ties and liberate yourself in a Soulgasm; a divine pinnacle of change.

When a person is ready for change they are ready to put down the distorted perceptions of the past and the need to prove themselves to others. They are also no longer bound to believe in what someone told them they need to be. A person who is truly ready for c s where they are emotionally, physically, and spiritually as the place that is not their final destination. This person has embodied a strong desire to do something about it the turmoil they experience; turmoil people may or may not be able to see. A woman who is truly ready for change is ready to experience a birthing transformation.

A transformational change can indeed equate to newness, but is not exclusive to needing new things. If you allow your transformation to level itself at the attainment of new (material) things you have willingly put your soul in the captivity of things with no substance. No one or thing should have that kind of power over your life. Holding onto your father's absence, mother's disapproval or grandmothers mean nature, will not induce your change event. It will abort it, miss carry it because your spiritual body was toxic, or it may cause you to feel rushed in birthing out your destiny; ushering you into depression. Take a moment to think about the things that have got in the way and prevented the fullness of your transformation. Is there anything you could have done differently? Here's one thing that never gets old, reject the title of being a victim because you are not a victim to the ways of old. You are a beautiful woman whose spirit is being guided towards the alignment of your Creators design! Forget about what they told you that you were or what the judged and labeled you as, you are the gem of creation! The apple of God's eye, fearfully and wonderful [illegible] ne structure, neurology, cognitive ability-EVERYTHING was created with intent and flawless design. God made no mistakes in his thought of who you are and who you are going to be. As you live out the rest your life try to tap into the workmanship of your Creator!

If you've made the mistake of attaching yourself to a negative soul tie, acknowledge it, forgive yourself and work diligently to detach yourself from it. Your soul is depending on it!

CONFRONTING THE GENERATIONAL SOUL

Have you ever felt like the odd ball out in your family? Maybe you feel like the one that's a little different. Do those feelings sound familiar? Not necessarily better or worse, but just different. Maybe you are the type of woman that gravitates to a particular culture or age group or gender that is different than your own. Is that you?

Under those circumstances, it can sometimes feel uncomfortable to be you, right? Especially when you begin to actually tap into the truth your soul holds in contrast to the current environment your soul lives in. Then, there is an even greater level of separation and position of discomfort. It might almost feel like the baby who sits in a soiled diaper waiting to be changed. It can even make [illegible] confidence seem to live miles away from one another. However you may want to pay attention to this feeling of different. In more cases than not, the truth is-YOU ARE different. The question that remains then is what will you do about it? Will you ignore that feeling? Will you hide it? Or will you find ways to embrace the evident need for eminent change?

If it hasn't been easy for you to make a change, what you may be up against is a spiritual battle. A soul, like a child, needs to be fed. What you feed your soul determines its development and its makeup. Furthermore your soul's development breeds off of what is familiar. Therefore the change you make on a soul level needs to be proverbial; even to itself, in order for your change to be sustained. Otherwise spiritual strongholds will keep your soul conflicted. For example, consider the natural body. Your natural body will give you a response if you decide to introduce it to unfamiliar eating patterns. So, if you are a person who has refrained from eating pork and all of a sudden you begin eating it, your body may reject it. The rejection is not necessarily due to the pork not being good for you, NO! The rejection is more about that type of food now being foreign to your body. Your body like your soul gets stronger from familiar patterns; the routine you are consistent to keep up with, not from foreign (unfamiliar) activity. So you must be loyal to feed your soul what is positive; learn to make posit[illegible] l into defeat.

The purpose of a stronghold is to keep you bound. Strongholds survive in confinement; they are the chain and link to the weights that make you feel like you can't be free. It is their job to work hard to keep you detained; they live for your destruction. Their ploys are presented attempts to get you to feed them anything negative, just to keep them alive. So if you find yourself in a place of repeat; always watching pornography, always over eating, always feeling emotional, always looking for love in all the wrong places-stop feeding the stronghold! Let those strongholds die of starvation. Do not be deceived, you still have the option to turn and walk away; break free of the stronghold. You still have time to stop feeding it the things that resemble its corruptness. You can do it, even when you can't change your environment including location and people.

In a perfect world, the mechanics within the world of change would permit you to change location and start fresh, new place new people. But how do you change when you don't live in a perfect world? What do you do when you can't readily change your environment because your kids just started school or you just bought a house or your friends disagree or your spouse doesn't want to move? Should you quit your transformation? In all honesty the choice is y[illegible]tion even if it looks like the only reasonable choice.

Take extreme precaution with how you define your soul outside of the diameter of where your soul infinitely lives; in the universal possibilities of opportunity. Too many women abort their destined purpose due to an identity crisis because in limited understanding they have allowed their identity to be defined as something outside of their own race, culture, or gender just to fit within the societal expectations of what a transformation "should" look like. Let your soul's spirit serve as the compass that navigates your soul's transformation.

When you look at the reality of your environment it can leave you feeling stuck, broken winged-unable to soar. However while you are a product of your environment, you do not have to be a carbon copy of it. Some products are best produced in intense situations. The key to note is that you are responsible for the product of your life by how your soul and spirit decides to live it.

Even if your mother or father was a rolling stone, or your environment bleeds with injustice, poverty, murder, abuse, and the like is not the determining factor of your destiny. You are! Your soul can rise up, out and above the tumultuous of situations because you; your soul and spirit are unlimited by the confines of circumstance contrary to the divine nature in which your soul was created to live. The Creator wired your soul and spirit to soar and win. But the choice is yours? How will you choose?

Tips and Helpful Hints for You to Remember

- You are a soul you do not need a soul.
- You have a spirit and your spirit is how you relate to God.
- The way you preserve your soul is by protecting your spirit.
- Despite your soul's environment you have the power to decide to change it.

Meditate on this:

"Come to me, all who are weary and heavy-laden, and I will give you rest. 'Take my yoke upon you, and learn from me, for I am gentle and humble in heart; and you shall find rest for your souls...'"

Matthew 11:28-30

Repeat this Affirmation of Encouragement:

My soul is divine and my spirit is connected to the light that illuminates truth.

A Tip for Nicky...

Let your soul lead you toward your spirit and away from the limitations life has presented you.

Soul food for thought:

Without judging Nicky, can you see yourself in her position or relate to some of her life choices or her story? Using Nicky as an example, take a moment to think about some of the ways you can confront and reflect on the following:

1. What is the importance of YOUR soul?
2. Who are the influences of your soul's make-up?
    1. Are they people, places, things, feelings etc...?
3. When did you first become aware of your spirit?
    2. Have you ever had an experience?
4. Where does your soul and spirit seem to be taking you?
5. Does it appear that Nicky is aware of her soul? Her spirit?
6. How aware are you to your soul?
7. How connected are you to your spirit?

Soulgasm

RELEASING YOUR SOUL TO LIVE

A Soulgasm is an inward turn of awareness conscious of morality and the responsibility of personal humanity. The Soulgasm experience wages war between the differences of what you're told to be and what you were created to be, by inspiring a voyage of the latter. It is a pure spiritual event where the sound of the ultimate power of God manifests the cosmic energy your soul soars in and gives birth to as a reality here in the earth realm.

The energy of cosmoses; the universe, bonds the galaxies, planets and the order of human nature as the life force that God gives in expansion of our consciousness. It is the playing ground and hearing aid of when your soul soars and when it cries liken to the event of childbirth.

SOULGASM

There is great beauty in the event of child birth. As a woman with child, you carry a person inside of you; a living being. Even before birth, this person will breathe and think and function inside of you as the child develops; beautiful growth, that comes with beautiful pain. Child birth can be the most excruciating pain a woman can ever physically feel and put her body through. Such pain births the most beautiful creation. The pain, although it births beauty, can make you cry. Think about the birthing event. A woman's legs are secure or held up and open as far as humanly possible. Then the doctor or midwife inserts their hand inside of her body to ensure the baby in labor will arrive safely. The Soulgasm experience is like the doctor in this scenario; ensuring the purposeful destiny that you carry is delivered safely.

What about you? You may not have had a soulgasmic experience before, but have you ever felt yourself in an emotional labor of sorts? Meaning, can you think about a time when you were in grave pain because you were in a situation of pure devastation? Despite the terrible nature of your experience, didn't you want to just break out? You might have cut or colored your hair, or got a makeover or pierced your nose or got a tattoo or slept with lots of men! Whatever you decided to do, the attempt was to birth a new y s that you knew was inside of you or that you just discovered. It probably felt like it was going to burst out of you if you didn't let it out in some way shape or form. You were vulnerable, yet at your strongest point, pivotal, monumental right? Right in that moment, between breakdown and breakout; the desire, the need for a deeper change is the exact pivotal moment of when it is time for a Soulgasm.

Your soulgasmic experience is as intimate as sex with your spouse. It will run deep, digging through time, age and dimensions chipping off the things that weigh you down spiritually and clipping off the things that will keep you from flying, from soaring as your soul was designed to do.

THE SOULGASMIC TECHNIQUE

During a sexual experience at the climax of your gasm, your body is quickened to a change; change in breathing patterns, change in body color, change in temperature, and change in energy; exhaustion and a need for rest and recovery. With your soul in mind, what if you gave it the same experience?

Eighty percent[3] of women are so accustomed to faking an

[3] According to a study conducted by Dr. Gayle Brewer of the University of Central

orgasm pri gasm is like! As a result these women find themselves externally going through motions but internally are feeling unfulfilled, unhappy, and off purpose. Every woman wants to fulfill her partner to climax and receive the same; it was designed that way on purpose. But if you are a woman who falls into the category of faking an orgasm, you are not in need of more sex or a different partner; you are in need of something deeper. You need a Soulgasm!

How different would your entire life be if you stopped pretending your soul and spirit was satisfied with life and actually allowed yourself to experience life in the depth and reach of a soulgasmic state? What do you have to lose from trying? Here are the Soulgasm techniques that you can use to begin your journey.

1. Protect it.
    1. Preserving the moment you enter into the spiritual gateway of the universe is essential. This is a holy and divine moment; it must be covered, it must be protected. Therefore, pray a prayer that invites God's divinity, his angels and Holy Spirit to protect and cover you in the moment you are released into the universe. As much as this is good, there is also an adversary. Be careful to honor the highest power,

---

Lancashire and Dr. Colin A. Hendrie of the University of Leeds

God and the “ying and yang” of the spirit realm.

2. Envision it.
    1. If you can see it, it can happen. Using the faculty of the mind through the power of rumination will help you to practice seeing what it is and where it is you want to be. It will help you to see your life in full color. Setting the stage for rumination in and of itself requires stillness. That means eyes closed, no moving, no thinking about other things and most importantly no sleeping, even if you get sleepy while doing this. Do your best to stop the inner and outer chatter of your mind. Within the Soulgasm technique there are no mantras, just pure relaxation. You will need to also be posture conscience. One way to ensure posture is through crossing your legs, with your back erect and fingers clasped for symmetrical balance.

3. Breathe through it.
    1. It will be easy to pick up a breathing chant; however this will not help you. The goal within breathing in the Soulgasm technique is to perform conscious

breathing; simple inhaling and exhaling on your SOULGASM ; more would require too much thought and defeat the event.

4. Envelope it.
    1. Perhaps you've had a few bad partners and so you learned that in order to "get yours" you must jump right in and get right to it. Within this part of the Soulgasm technique that strategy will not work for you; you will not climax. For this reason some women may find this step the most difficult. But the goal here is to embrace the moment. Stay there, still, holding, breathing naturally. You must find the patience of…waiting for it…waiting for it. …waiting for it. …then relaxing in it; the moment.

5. Embrace it.
    1. This part of embracing it is not relative to the moment, it's referring to embracing you, the real you. The you that is going to begin to come forward, full circle. Don't choose to rebel against what you begin to see, it may be ugly. When you choose rebellion, really what you are choosing to neglect the potential and design of your being. Therefore enjoy the discovery embracing you will

unfold.

6. Recognize it.
    1. In this moment of stillness, awareness, and openness you may feel led to say something, not chatter, something of substance, if it comes to you, let it flow. Be aware that when you speak you will be speaking in the echoes of the universe so your voice may sound different, unrecognizable, yet refreshing. When you hear the power in the sound of your voice you may be taken aback. Don't run out of the room! Recognize it, acknowledge the power in your voice and begin to speak life. Speak out loud what your soul desires. In the moment of being in the spirit talk with your Creator and charge the universe to respond and get used to the power in your voice. The power you hold in this moment can command destiny to manifest right before your eyes; flow with it.

7. Burst in its excitement.
    1. As your soul is flowing in the spirit and commanding the very angels in heaven; charging

the universe, don't be afraid of the BOOM your soul SOULGASM It's going to climax, it's going to be huge, but it's necessary.

8. Sleep in it.

    1. You very well may be worn out by this point. But when you go to bed, it will be the best sleep you've ever had in your life! Sleep will rejuvenate and enhance the power of the body, mind and intellect. Rest up and rest well for your next Soulgasmic experience; a divine encounter that will release the unhindered awareness of a pure conscious and spiritual communion with God.

The expected length of a Soulgasm experience is undetermined because how long you are in the moment of a Soulgasm is completely up to your performance. It can go as long or short as you like, but it will only flow as long as you allow it to. It is recommended that you allow yourself to experience it as much as needed; it is for your full benefit.

The fundamental beauty of a woman's soul is a reality desperately in need of cultural infiltration, so often bereft of paternity and maternity on a spiritual level. The more a woman can understand the dimensions of her soul, get in tune with her Creator and exude the confident esteem she innately embodies, the more healthy relat)f her soul will shine through her to them and the world.

As a woman, you are a beautiful creature interwoven with individual personality, focus and desire; divine architecture-you are a goddess in your own right! Don't be guilty of wasting your God given spiritual dexterity on the toxins life can present to you. You can avoid such guilt by always remembering that you are built strong, you are precious, you are invaluable, and irresistible. Lady friend, for once in your life make the decision to use those powers to give birth to the unstoppable nature of your mind, body, soul and spirit!

Think about it this way, when you are in the zone of a sexual climax; what can get in the way of that moment? Absolutely NOTHING! Why because you won't let it! The same applies to life. When you are experiencing a Soulgasm be careful not to let anything stand in the way of it. Not emotions, not social or economic circumstance, and surely not a man, another woman or even yourself, to get in the way. There is no excuse great enough to stand in the way of you elevating to a spiritually gasmic stratosphere because it will only be to your detriment if you miss today's opportunity to inhale, exhale and Soulgasm.

Tips and Helpful Hints for You to Remember

- You hold the divinity of birth; the beauty of life.
- Your spirit is the power in which your soul soars and "gasm's."
- A perpetual re-visitation of your personal Soulgasm technique will serve as an enhancement as your being evolves.

Meditate on this:

"You are altogether beautiful, my darling, and there is no blemish in you...'"

Song of Songs 4:7

Repeat this Affirmation of Encouragement:

The nature of my being is beauty, peace and fragrant in love; the authenticity of its scent brings life to all who encounter it.

A Tip for Nicky...

Never allow negative people or negative circumstances to bind the infinity of your soul and spirits power together. The power in their differences is what keeps them inseparably charged.

Soul food for thought:

What are some of the ways you can improve your
Soulgasmic technique?

____

____

____

____

____

Woman to woman and without judgment, what advice would you give Nicky for her next chapter in life?

____

____

____

Sealing the deal

A TIME TO PRAY

To the most powerfully gracious God and Father I submit myself to your omniscient presence. I welcome you into this moment, thankfully. I am asking for a special blessing to rest upon those who have read this book and hear your voice. Allow the words that have been spoken to erect a revelation for a greater inner transformation. Thank you for bringing each and every reader to a place where their very soul will experience the essence of your power; in order to know you (and themselves) more clearly.

Dear Lord, please protect their decision to open up to a soulgasmic experience by saturating the atmosphere of each and every one of their circumstances with your holy love; sealing the rest of their lives with peace and prosperity. Thank you for these blessings in advance.

Amen!

INHALE EXHALE

&

Soulgasm!

Don't miss these other titles by:

YOLANDA LEWIS

Available for order at:

www.extremeoverflow.com/#!books/cnec

References

1. Inspirational Quotes. (2012) http://www.beliefnet.com/Inspiration/Inspiration-Quotes.aspx#ixzz221piR0fl
2. Young, T., Neghash S., & Long, R. (2009). Enhancing sexual desire and intimacy via the metaphor of a problem child: utilizing structural-strategic therapy. Journal of Sex & Marital Therapy, 35(5), 402-417.doi:10.1080/00926230903065971
3. Greenberg, L. S., & Mateu Marques, C. (1998). Emotions in couples systems. *Journal of Systemic Therapies, 17*, 93–107.
4. The American Heritage Dictionary www.thefreedictionary.com
5. Berke JD, et al. "Addiction, Dopamine, and the Molecular Mechanisms of Memory," *Neuron* (March 2000): Vol. 25, No. 3, pp. 515–32.
6. Crabbe JC. "Genetic Contributions to Addiction," *Annual Review of Psychology* (2002): Vol. 53, pp. 435–62.
7. Hyman SE. "A 28-Year-Old Man Addicted to Cocaine," *Journal of the American Medical Association* (Nov. 28, 2001): Vol. 286, No. 20, pp. 2586–94.
8. Hyman SE. "Why Does The Brain Prefer Opium to Broccoli?" *Harvard Review of Psychiatry* (May-June 1994): Vol. 2, No. 1, pp. 43–46.
9. Koob GF, et al. "Neurobiological Mechanisms in the Transition from Drug Use to Drug Dependence," *Neuroscience and Biobehavioral Reviews* (Jan. 2004): Vol. 27, No. 8, pp. 739–49.
10. Nestler EJ. "Total Recall – the Memory of Addiction," *Science* (June 22, 2001): Vol. 292, No. 5525, pp. 2266–67.
11. McMinn, M. R. (1996). *Psychology, theology, and spirituality in Christian counseling.* Carol Stream, IL: Tyndale House.
12. Hunter, Anina, (2010) CBS News http://www.cbsnews.com/news/ouch-80-percent-of-women-faking-orgasms-says-study/

32075693R00121

Made in the USA
Charleston, SC
02 August 2014